Penny Dreadful

ALSO BY LAUREL SNYDER

Any Which Wall

Up and Down the Scratchy Mountains

Inside the Slidy Diner (picture book)

Penny
Dreadful

LAUREL SNYDER

DRAWINGS BY
ABIGAIL HALPIN

RANDOM HOUSE ⌂ NEW YORK

A line from "Dream Song 14" from *The Dream Songs* by John Berryman, copyright © 1969 by John Berryman, renewed 1997 by Kate Donahue Berryman (New York: Farrar, Straus & Giroux, LLC, 1969), appears on page 6.

Visit us on the Web! www.randomhouse.com/kids

Educators and librarians, for a variety of teaching tools,
visit us at www.randomhouse.com/teachers

Visit www.laurelsnyder.com

Library of Congress Cataloging-in-Publication Data
Snyder, Laurel.
Penny Dreadful / Laurel Snyder. — 1st ed.
p. cm.
Summary: When her father suddenly quits his job, the almost-ten-year-old, friendless Penny and her neglectful parents leave their privileged life in the city for a ramshackle property in Thrush Junction, Tennessee, where their tenants have never paid rent and the town's shops include Praise God the Lord Hot Dog Shack and Fugate's Feed Shop and Bridal Store.
ISBN 978-0-375-86199-4 (trade) —
ISBN 978-0-375-96199-1 (lib. bdg.) —
ISBN 978-0-375-89346-9 (e-book)
[1. Country life—Tennessee—Fiction. 2. Family life—Tennessee—Fiction.
3. Resourcefulness—Fiction.] I. Title.
PZ7.S6851764Pe 2010
[Fic]—dc22
2009032104

Printed in the United States of America
10 9 8 7 6 5 4 3 2 1
First Edition

For Mose and Lewis—my *everything change*

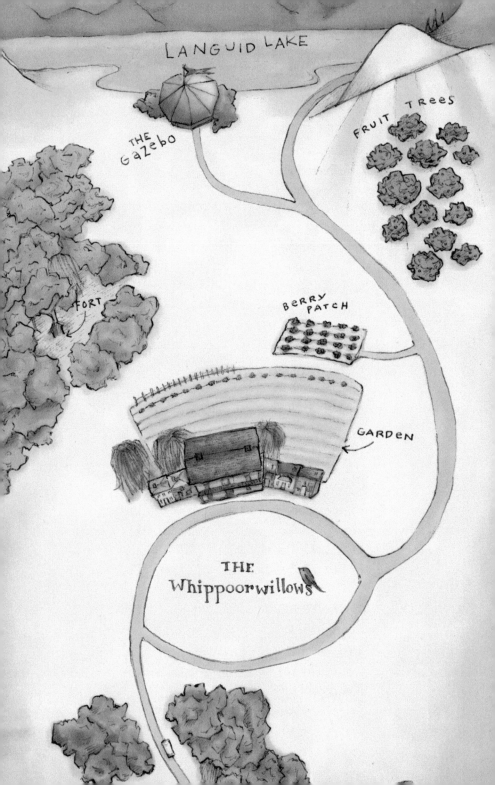

CONTENTS

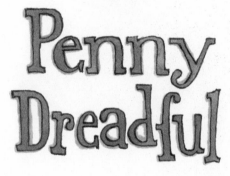

BOOK ONE

HEAVY BORED

EVER TO CONFESS YOU'RE BORED

Penelope Grey knew she was lucky. She lived in a big stone mansion in the greatest city on earth, with a canopy over her bed, wonderful books to read, and lots of toys to play with. Her parents were delightful people. Her father was funny and her mother was sweet, and they both loved Penelope very much—of this she was certain. Unfortunately, she didn't get to actually *see* her parents all that often, since her father tended to be busy with his important job at the top of a very tall building, and her mother had any number of social obligations and deserving charities that kept her tied up most days.

Still, Penelope knew she was lucky. She had a chef to prepare her meals and an extremely capable tutor named Joanna who taught her interesting things each day in the comfort of her very own home. She had occasional supervised outings to the zoo or the park, accompanied by pleasant girls with names like Jane and Olivia. She had a housekeeper, so she never had to pick up her room, and she had no grubby little brothers or sisters. It was all very tidy.

Yes, Penelope knew she had nothing to complain about. She had everything a girl could want. Unfortunately, knowing that she *should* be happy only made it worse that Penelope was not happy at all.

The truth was that Penelope was bored. Bored in a terrible, empty, ongoing, forever kind of way that made her sigh much more deeply than any ten-year-old girl should ever sigh. She was bored with the delicious meals and the polite playmates. She was bored with her great, echoing house. She was even bored with her name— Penelope Geraldine Grey—which she thought sounded like the name of an old lady with too many diamond rings and not enough hair. She was bored with her hazel eyes and her medium-length brown hair, which was not quite straight and not quite curly, and could not have been more boring. And when she caught herself thinking about all of this, she was bored with herself, which was worst of all.

This sorry state of affairs was only made more awful by the fact that Penelope had read enough books (they were just about the only thing that Penelope did *not* find boring) to know that bored little girls who live in mansions are usually spoiled. Penelope did *not* want to be spoiled. Spoiled girls in books were silly and selfish. Still, Penelope could not help it. Whatever she did, wherever she went, she was horribly, hungrily bored.

Penelope thought that perhaps things might improve in a few years, if only she could go away to boarding school. In books, boarding school was always very exciting, full of deep secrets and midnight escapades, and sometimes magic. But even if her parents agreed, *that* was still far off in the future, and in the meantime she could think of no other real solution to her problem.

One drizzly Saturday afternoon in May, Penelope was sitting on the window seat in the marble foyer at the front of the house. She had just finished reading the very last Anne of Green Gables book, and she was depressed at the thought of what to do *next*. She watched strangers pass by the front window in the spitting rain with their umbrellas, and she made a game of trying to guess which stranger might look up and smile or nod. So far, at least fifty people had passed, and not a single one had looked up at her from the wet pavement. Penelope was just about to stop playing the game when her father came down the stairs. He plunked himself beside Penelope on the wide window seat.

"You're looking a little down in the mouth. What's wrong, sport?" Dirk Grey asked his daughter in his usual jovial way.

"I'm *bored*, Daddy," admitted Penelope with a slump and a sigh.

Dirk pondered this for a moment. "Hmm." Then he cleared his throat, stuck an index finger theatrically into the air, and quoted at the ceiling, "Ever to confess you're bored means you have no Inner Resources!"

Penelope looked at her father quizzically. "What's that mean?" she asked.

"It means that when you're bored, you need to think of something to *do*," answered her father. "It means you can't blame boredom on anyone but yourself. You can't just wait for things to happen to you. You have to *do* things. Or anyway, I think that's what it means. It's often hard to tell with poetry!"

Then he stood back up and headed off in the direction of the kitchen, leaving Penelope to think sulkily that it hadn't sounded much like poetry to her.

Even so, she was glad to have some advice to follow, and she took her father's words to heart. From that day on, she tried to *do* things every single day. Since she had little experience with *doing*, and didn't know where to begin, she turned to her books for help. Each morning she stood in front of her bookshelf with her eyes squeezed tightly shut and ran a finger down the spines of the bindings, stopping whenever the mood struck her. Then she'd pull out that particular book, flip to a random page, and do whatever the people in that book happened to be doing.

In this way, Penelope succeeded in exploring her (dusty) attic, planting some (cucumber) seeds, inventing her own secret language, starting a diary, roller-skating up and down the halls of the Grey mansion, putting on a puppet show (though there was nobody but Josie, the housekeeper, to watch it), and a handful of other fun-sounding things.

One day, inspired by a book called *A Little Princess*, Penelope asked her mother to invite Jane (or Olivia, if Jane was busy; it didn't much matter) over to spend the night. She requested that Chef fill the fridge with his special triple-deluxe chocolate cheesecake squares, in expectation of a candlelit midnight feast. But when, around midnight, Penelope tried to rouse Jane with a flashlight to tiptoe downstairs "like poor orphans," Jane stared silently up at Penelope from her sleeping bag in a way that made Penelope feel instantly bad.

"What's wrong?" asked Penelope. "What did I say?"

"I *was* an orphan, Penelope," said Jane. "In Russia.

Before I came to America to live with my parents." Then, without saying anything else, Jane buried her face in her pillow and went to sleep.

This left Penelope feeling terrible for Jane, and guilty about her blunder, but also bewildered that she'd known Jane for several years and never had any idea she was adopted. How had that happened?

Even with all her *doing,* Penelope remained bored. It was nice that on the nights when her mother was home to tuck her in, and she asked, "What did you do today, dear?" Penelope could answer her with something interesting, like "I made a piñata." But it didn't feel like enough.

The more she mulled the situation over, the more frustrated Penelope felt. In books kids did fun stuff, sure. But also big things happened. People died and were born. Fortunes were lost and found. Magic talismans turned up and houses disappeared in tornadoes, and Penelope could imagine no way to make any of that happen.

Yes, Penelope decided. *It is going to take something enormous for me to become unbored. It is going to take an everything change.* For that she figured she'd just have to wait.

Then one day after her finger stopped on a book called *Magic or Not?* Penelope wandered out into the perfectly manicured lawn of her backyard, holding a folded scrap of paper. There was a decorative wishing well of sorts in the middle of the Greys' lawn, beneath a little red maple tree. The well had been designed by a famous architect, and a picture of it was in a book her mother kept on the coffee table.

Penelope didn't think the well looked very wishable or magical. It was too fancy and nicely kept. Besides, she wasn't sure she believed in wishes anyway, but her finger (and the book) had determined what she must *do*, and so she would *do* it.

With an unfamiliar flutter in her chest, Penelope unfolded the scrap of paper and read what she'd written one last time.

I wish something interesting would happen
when I least expect it, just like in a book.

Penelope refolded her wish carefully and tossed it into the well. Then she leaned over and peered down after it.

The well was only about six feet deep. The cement floor had a small mesh grate set into it, and Penelope fully expected to see her wish sitting on that grate, but funnily enough, Penelope couldn't see her wish at all anymore. The well appeared to be completely empty.

That's odd, thought Penelope, leaning over to examine all the shadowed corners of the well's bottom. But the wish really did seem to have vanished, and after a few minutes Penelope straightened up and went inside, where nothing seemed any different at all.

So Penelope forgot about her wish. Mostly.

2

THE EVERYTHING CHANGE

About a week later Penelope was sunk deep in a red leather chair in the library of the Grey mansion, quietly reading a book full of unfortunate events, when suddenly she heard the front door slam open in the foyer one room over.

Penelope looked up, dropped her book, and climbed out of her big chair. She ran to a set of open French doors. On the other side of them she found her father looking decidedly wild-eyed, leaning against a wall. He was clutching a cardboard box full of papers.

Dirk Grey dropped his box on the shiny floor of the foyer, where it made a thunderous noise as it hit the marble. "I've had it! I did it! I'm done!" he shouted in a ragged voice, which echoed against the polished stone. He didn't seem to have noticed Penelope.

She started to head toward him, but then, for some

reason, she changed her mind. Instead, she ducked behind one of the doors and watched as Dirk ran his hands through his thick hair in a desperate kind of way. He shook his head from side to side so that the hair stuck out all over. It looked funny, but Penelope, hidden behind the smoked glass panel of the French door, did not laugh. She held her breath. There was something in her father's posture, his strange glazed stare, that held her still and silent. She had no experience with this sort of situation, and no idea what to say. She could almost feel the questions hanging in the air, the *maybe*, the *what if?*

What happens now? she wondered. With prickles on the back of her neck, Penelope tried to breathe without making a sound.

Just then Penelope's mother, Delia, emerged from the kitchen at the back of the house. "Done what, darling?" she called out in a lilting voice as her heels clicked across the marble floor. In a second she had joined her husband, holding a cookbook. Delia Grey didn't like to cook, but she was very good at planning meals. (Chef took care of the rest.)

When Delia saw the state her husband was in, her cookbook fell to the floor with a *thwop*. "Darling?" she asked, rushing over. "Are you—all right?"

"I'm better than that!" said Dirk, looking at her with a strange gleam in his eyes. "I'm great! I'm free! I quit my

job!" he shouted, though there was no need to yell anymore since Delia was standing right in front of him. Dirk reached out for her hands and danced her around on the slick floor in a manic way, so that *her* usually perfect hair stood on end too. "Isn't that wonderful? Hurrah! I'm free! Let's celebrate. Where's the champagne? Chef!" Chef didn't appear.

Penelope watched through the gap in the French doors as Delia extricated herself from the unexpected polka to step back and stare at her husband. She spit out a mouthful of her dark blond hair and whispered in a worried way, "Dirk—you aren't *serious?*"

"Serious as a heart attack," he said with a wide smile. "A heart attack I won't have to have anymore since I quit my job!"

Penelope listened intently through the doors. This was by far the most interesting thing that had ever happened. Even better than the time all the power went out and they had to light candles in the bathrooms. This, now, might just be her *everything change!* Penelope remembered her wish and felt chills run down her spine, exactly like in all the books. She stared at her parents as though they were acting out the last scene in a very good movie.

Delia frowned. "What exactly do you mean by *quit?*"

"What does it sound like I mean?" said Dirk. "I mean

that I went to work today like usual, but then I changed my mind. I hate Grey Investments!" He scowled.

"Now. Dirk. Dear. I think you're overreacting," said Delia in a cool tone. She planted a calm hand on her husband's arm. "You don't hate it. Maybe you find it tedious some days, but you don't really hate it. You'll feel differently tomorrow."

Penelope watched as her father considered this for a second.

"Nope," he said with certainty. "I *hate* it. I have for a long time. I just kept my mouth shut until now. I didn't see any need to concern you, didn't want to make any waves. But today—today I snapped. I couldn't keep it bottled up any longer. I hate everything about that place. It's boring and cold, and—and heartless."

Heartless! Penelope hung on every word.

"But, Dirk," said Delia, "even if you don't exactly love the job, it's your family's company. You can't just walk away from—"

"Family, shmamily!" cried Dirk, exasperated. "If my parents—God rest their souls—are really watching me from heaven above, don't you think they want me to be happy? They probably understand better than anyone how soul-crushing that place is. Can't *you?*"

Soul-crushing! Silently, Penelope cheered for her father.

She understood! Penelope didn't know much about her father's job, and she didn't exactly like the idea of her parents fighting, but she did know a thing or two about dull. If her father's job was as bad as he said it was, Penelope didn't see why he *shouldn't* quit.

Dirk ran his hand through his hair again and continued. "Besides, I was no good at the job anyway." Dirk looked at his feet sadly as he said this, before gazing up at the vaulted ceiling with a wrinkled forehead. "Sorry, Mum. Sorry, Pop. I didn't mean to let you down."

Penelope's mother seemed to melt. She reached out a hand to smooth her husband's hair. "Oh, darling, you haven't let anyone down," she said. "You're a wonderful success! You're president of the company, after all."

Penelope was glad to see her mother soften, but Dirk didn't seem to appreciate it. He looked over and flashed his wife a wry smile. "It's called *Grey* Investments, Delia, and I'm the only Grey left. I don't think my natural aptitude has much to do with my distinguished title."

Delia frowned slightly at this. She planted her fists firmly on her hips. "I was *trying* to be nice. Are you just determined to feel bad today?"

"No," said Dirk gruffly. "In fact, I was feeling excited. Until I started talking to you. Humph."

Delia glared crossly at Dirk, who glared right back.

For a while neither of them said anything, and the room was full of a strange silence. Penelope frowned. She wished she could tell her father that *she* understood, but it seemed a bad time to interrupt.

Finally Delia made an exasperated face. "Well, I'm *sorry*, Dirk. But how did you expect me to react? You come home and tell me you've quit your job of nearly twenty years when it happens to be our only regular source of income. It's something of a shock."

"Sorry," he said. "But the money will work itself out. It always does, and I really wanted you to be excited with me. This isn't a bad thing, Delia. It's a good thing. *I* think so, anyway. Can't you be happy too?"

Delia didn't reply.

Penelope watched her parents fall silent again through the gap in the doors. She wondered if the silence was the end of the conversation. It didn't *feel* like the end. It didn't seem like anything had been finished yet.

Suddenly Penelope sneezed! It was a small sneeze, but still it was a sneeze.

Delia's eyes flew to the library doors. "Penelope?" she called out sharply. "Penelope Grey? Are you in there?"

Penelope grimaced and took a deep breath. She stuck her head out and whispered faintly, "Yes, Mother. I kind of am."

"Were you listening to us?" asked Delia, glancing at Dirk and then back at Penelope. She looked concerned. "You shouldn't be. This is grown-up talk. Not for young ears."

"Sorry, Mother," said Penelope.

"Would you be so kind as to close the door and give us a few minutes alone?" asked Delia. She phrased this as a question, but her tone made it pretty clear to Penelope that she had no choice in the matter.

"Okay," said Penelope meekly, shutting the French doors.

Once she was out of sight again, she put her ear to the cold glass. Her parents' hushed voices rose and fell steadily in the next room, but Penelope couldn't make out a thing they said. It was infuriating! At last something was happening, and she was left out. But it was frustrating to eavesdrop unsuccessfully, so eventually Penelope gave up. She headed back to her book, in which a baby was sure to bite someone shortly. Penelope thought *she* might like to bite someone too.

After a while the hum of voices died away, and Penelope went to the glass doors. Then, slowly, she opened the doors a crack and peeked out. She was just in time to see Dirk head up the stairs with his box. Delia stood at the bottom step and gripped the banister tightly as she called out in a pleading voice, "But, Dirk, what is it you plan to do now?"

After a moment Dirk turned on the landing and paused. He looked back over his shoulder and his voice tumbled down the stairs. "Long ago," he said, with a faraway look in his eyes, "I liked to write stories. One of my teachers said I was good at it. He said I should try my hand at a novel, but my father convinced me it was a silly thing to do. So I didn't even try."

"You wrote stories?" asked Delia with interest. "I didn't know that."

Penelope could tell that her mother was trying to be nice, but Dirk only shrugged. "There are *lots* of things you don't know," he said coldly, before disappearing into his office and closing the door.

"I guess maybe that's true," whispered Delia, her shoulders hunched in a sad way.

For the next few weeks Dirk wandered around the house in his bathrobe, clutching a cup of cold coffee and muttering, with a pencil stuck behind his ear. The messy box of papers found a home on the desk in his study. When Penelope eagerly peeked in to ask him how his book was coming, he looked up and said slowly, "Fine— I guess."

Although she was a little concerned about her father's

lack of continued enthusiasm, Penelope decided this must just be what writers did. Mostly she liked having Dirk around, even if he was being kind of weird. Sometimes they took a father-daughter walk together in the morning to get the paper from the newsstand down the street. It was nice, and a little different.

But Penelope wondered when things would begin to be *really* different. In books, *everything changes* were followed by all sorts of other exciting developments. Unfortunately, for the most part, Penelope's life went on as usual. Each morning she ate a bowl of cereal and a quarter of a honeydew melon by herself. Then she spent the day with Joanna, learning about the American Revolution or decimals or something else useful, because there's no summer vacation when you have a tutor.

As Dirk muttered and puttered, Delia wiped flower petals discreetly off the shiny surface of the dining room table and oversaw the staff. But Penelope noticed that her mother wasn't smiling or singing nearly as often as usual. She also noticed that her parents didn't appear to be talking to each other very much. *That* was a little concerning.

Then one day Freddie the driver suddenly wasn't there. This didn't affect Penelope much since she rarely went anywhere in the car, but when Chef disappeared a week later, Penelope had to wonder what was going on.

Chef's absence had a considerable effect on Penelope's life. Not only did Delia not enjoy cooking, she turned out not to be very good at it, as evidenced by a parade of terrible dinners, including a very burnt stir-fry, an undercooked roast chicken, and a platter of unpleasant cheeseburgers, which Penelope found especially incredible. She wouldn't have guessed it was possible to ruin a cheeseburger, but she didn't want to hurt her mother's feelings, so she just chewed each bite as quickly as possible and drank a lot of milk.

Penelope was beginning to be sorry about her well-wish and its dismal aftermath, if that was what all of this was. She hadn't been sure if she believed in magic before, *really*, but—

Then one evening, after another nearly silent dinner of little rolled-up things that she guessed were supposed to be enchiladas, Penelope decided it was time to take matters into her own hands. Somehow, her generally boring life was turning into a silent, tense, stressful boring life. Something needed to be done. After standing in her room examining her bookcase for inspiration and pondering the problem at hand, Penelope struck upon a book—*The Penderwicks*—and a solution. The Greys needed a vacation!

Dirk had already disappeared into his office, and

Delia was sitting in the parlor writing something down on a notepad when Penelope found her. "Mother," she said as casually as she could, "I was thinking we need a change of scenery. A vacation. Maybe we could rent a rambling farmhouse in the country!"

Usually the Greys visited a very nice resort at the ocean in July, but Penelope found the idea of an old-fashioned trip to the country appealing. There would probably be county fairs and friendly locals and berry picking. Plus, the fresh air would surely help her parents' moods. Wasn't that what fresh air was for?

Delia appeared not to have even heard her daughter's suggestion. She looked lost in thought as she scribbled numbers on her pad. Periodically she consulted her checkbook.

"Mother?" Penelope tried again softly. Then louder, "Mother!"

This time Delia looked up. When she did, Penelope was shocked to find that there were tears standing in her mother's eyes. "Yes, Penelope?" Delia asked softly. "Did you need something, dear?"

"Oh," Penelope said, taken aback. "It's nothing," she mumbled. "I just—had an idea."

Delia set down her pen and asked without inflection, "What's that?"

Penelope hesitated. Suddenly her idea seemed silly, but she had already begun, and so she said, "Just—to go to the country, like in a book. But we can talk about it another time. It's really no big deal. Is—is everything okay?"

Delia smiled weakly, and with the back of a finger wiped away the tears that hadn't fallen. "Of course it is. Or anyway, it will be. But I don't—I *don't* think we can afford to go to the country, or the beach, or anywhere else. Not this year. Maybe next summer?"

Penelope nodded slowly, absorbing what her mother had just said. Not afford it? The Greys always went away to the beach in July! They had rented the same ocean-view suite every year since Penelope could remember. Penelope stared into her mother's sad eyes, and suddenly she understood. This was bad. This was serious. If the Greys could not afford to go to the beach, things must not be okay.

"Sure," she said at last. "Next year. Or—not. I mean—it doesn't matter," she continued, fumbling.

"That's my good girl," said Delia.

Penelope tried to smile, but the smile got stuck halfway. It felt awkward, false.

"And, Penelope?" added Delia. "Please don't mention anything to your father about this. Let's have this be our secret for now. I don't want to worry him with unpleasant money talk. Not until he's feeling a little more—himself."

Penelope nodded again, slowly, and felt her fake smile slip into a frown. She had thought her parents were mad at each other, because of the not talking, but that wasn't the case. Her mother's voice sounded kind, and she didn't look angry so much as worried and tired.

Delia sighed. "It's just, he's going through a rough patch, and I don't want to make things any harder for him. Though, honestly, I'm not quite sure how to manage things myself. I know we *will*, of course, but I'm not sure *how*, exactly. We're broke, I'm afraid."

Broke? Penelope hesitated. "But I thought," she said quietly, because it felt like a strange thing to say out loud, "we were—*rich*."

"Well," said Delia, "in a way we are." She seemed to be choosing her words carefully. "You see, your father's family has always been rather well-to-do, and your grandparents left us this house when they passed away, but the cost of the maintenance for a house like this is huge. There are so many bills each month, and the staff to pay. We really depended on your father's salary to keep everything going. Plus, I'm embarrassed to admit that we often spend more than he makes, which means a lot of credit cards, and that gets tricky, juggling all of them. I've already had to let Chef go, and Freddie too. Maybe you noticed?"

Penelope nodded.

"Oh, Penelope," Delia said, "I'm so sorry. I shouldn't talk about this with you at all, but I have to tell someone, and until your father is more himself . . ." Delia sighed. "Besides, I don't know how else to explain to you about why we can't have a vacation this year. Or anything else *extra*."

"It's okay," said Penelope. "There are probably a lot of bugs in the country anyway, and snakes." She patted Delia's shoulder.

And it *was* okay. Despite the weird seriousness of everything her mother was telling her, it felt strangely good to talk about it all. It felt nice to understand things a little better, to actually *know* instead of guessing.

She only hoped her well-wish hadn't caused this mess. This wasn't at all what she'd meant by *interesting*.

Delia looked at Penelope and sniffled. "I love you," she said. Then, without warning, she reached out to pull Penelope toward her. She folded her daughter up in a big startling hug.

Penelope, caught in the hug, felt many things all at once. Mostly it was just nice to be hugged, but underneath the warmth Penelope had the feeling that her pleasant, boring life, with her small family in their large stone house, had been until recently like a movie with the sound turned down low. Since she'd never been able to hear what anyone was saying, she'd just assumed things were fine, if dull. Suddenly it was as if someone had turned the sound up, and she was discovering that the story had complications.

"Everything will be fine, Mother," she said into Delia's warm shoulder. "Just wait and see. I bet things will be better again really soon."

Penelope thought that sounded right, like the sort of thing a daughter might say in a book.

3

PENELOPE OPENS THE DOOR

As it turned out, Penelope was dead wrong about things getting better. Because after that day things around the house only slipped further. Since she had no idea what to do about any of it, Penelope just watched it all fall, like rain through a window.

First, Joanna was given the summer off. When she politely asked why Penelope did not require summer instruction for the first time in seven years, Delia mumbled something about how Penelope was being sent to a special arts camp.

Of course, this was not the truth at all, and Penelope was startled to see her mother lie. She stared curiously at Delia, who looked at her feet until Joanna turned and left the room. Penelope had never especially liked Joanna, so it was with a bewildered sense of relief that she watched her tutor walk away from the house for good.

Shortly after that people began calling from fancy stores and credit card companies. Each time Penelope answered the phone and told whoever was at the other end of the line that her mother was away, they asked her to please tell Mrs. Delia Grey that she needed to call and discuss her bill. Penelope stopped answering the telephone.

Then one Thursday, Josie the housekeeper quit, saying that she absolutely refused to keep up with the trail of litter that Dirk left behind him as he wandered the house lost in thought. She stormed out, waving her hands in the air and yelling, "Crazy man! Owes three weeks' back pay and can't pick up his own socks! I am *not* your mother, and I don't have to put up with your mess anymore, thank goodness!"

Dirk ran after her, pleading. "I'm sorry, Josie! I'll wash my own coffee cups from now on! I'll stop walking on your wet floors, I promise!"

But Josie was gone, and that was a problem, because while managing the staff had always been Delia's job, managing the house itself wasn't something *any* of the Greys knew much about. It was a very large house—four giant floors, full of rooms—and it got away from them. Dishes piled up in the sink, once-shiny floors grew dim, and small mountains of clutter multiplied in rooms all over the house, though nobody said a word about it. Penelope tried to see the mess as an adventure, but it was really just plain depressing.

As the mess got worse, Penelope tried not to think about the wishing well. *It was just a silly game,* she told herself. *I didn't do this. I couldn't possibly have done this.*

On top of everything else, as June wore into July, the house also became unbearably hot. Penelope wasn't sure whether the air-conditioning was broken or Delia had shut it off to save money, but either way, Penelope didn't want to complain about it. So when the temperature became absolutely intolerable, she went down to the cellar with a flashlight to read in the darkness beneath the stairs. Though it was cooler there, sitting alone in the basement was really just a different kind of sad.

Through all of this, the Greys didn't snipe at each other or fight about whose turn it was to sweep up. Instead, Dirk and Delia walked around the house avoiding each other and closing the doors on any particularly messy rooms. Delia unplugged the phone and stopped singing to herself completely. In the evenings she sat on the couch in the dark and sipped what seemed to be an endless glass of white wine, alone. Dirk continued to mutter in his robe, read old newspapers, and drink cold coffee. Lightbulbs burned out, and the great stone mansion became a vast series of dark hallways and shut doors. It was as though the house had gone to sleep, and Penelope watched it all worriedly, wishing everyone would go back to their old, boring ways.

This might have remained the sorry state of things for a long, long time if, one afternoon, Dirk had not loaded the washing machine with seven towels, a pair of running shoes, and two bathroom rugs, so that it made an alarming *thumpity thumpity* noise and walked itself across the laundry room before it broke. At first Penelope and her parents simply ignored the piles of towels and clothes as they'd ignored everything else. They all pretended not to notice the gray mildewy smell hanging in the air. Then the piles of laundry turned into mountains, until *everything* in the house was dirty.

Penelope—worried into silence herself—tried very hard not to bother her parents, but the day she could not find a single clean pair of pants and was forced to wear the elephant costume from her dress-up trunk, she finally had to say *something*. She found her father, who was rooting through jars and bottles in the refrigerator looking for a snack.

"Daddy," she said cautiously, "I—I kind of need some pants."

"What's wrong with the ones you're wearing?" her father asked sharply, without removing his head from the refrigerator.

Penelope stared down at her wrinkly gray legs. She supposed Dirk didn't understand her need for clothes since he himself hadn't taken off his bathrobe in weeks. So she went into the upstairs study, where her mother was sitting at a rolltop desk staring blankly at a pile of long white envelopes.

"Mother, I could really use some—um—clean pants," said Penelope. She spoke softly and tried not to sound too demanding. She hated to bother her mother, who was nervously twirling her hair with a finger, but she *did* need pants.

"I know, dear," said Delia both guiltily and quietly, without looking up. "There are just so many things to do—how *do* people manage it all? I've been trying to remember what it was like before I married your father and got used to having so much help." She sighed. "I'm going to the Laundromat soon, I promise. Once I'm through making ends meet." She bravely tore open one of the envelopes.

Penelope looked down at her elephant legs and took a deep, brave breath. "Mother," she said gently. "I think maybe—maybe you need to do the laundry *first*. Maybe you need to do it *now*. Or at least show *me* how to do it."

Delia glanced up and registered that her daughter was dressed as a pachyderm. Then she looked down at her own pink shirt, which had been slightly spattered with burnt spaghetti sauce the day before. Her chin began to quiver. Two tears rolled down her cheeks. She wiped them away and tried to smile. "How did we come to this?" she whispered softly, setting down the envelope and looking at her lap. "How did this happen?"

Penelope wished she hadn't said anything. "I'm sorry, Mother," she said. "It's okay. I don't really need pants. These are fine." She swung her gray tail in what she hoped was a fun-loving gesture. "See?"

Delia stared at her daughter. Another tear dripped down her face.

"Are you okay?" asked Penelope, although the answer seemed horribly obvious.

Delia rubbed at her face, shook her head slightly, and then, with a strange, forced smile firmly in place, she said far too cheerfully, "Of *course*, dear. I'm always okay. Just a minute. I just need a quick minute alone."

Delia ran from the room.

Penelope heard a door slam, followed by the sound of sobbing. She'd made her mother *cry*! What had she done? *Why* had she opened her stupid mouth?

She turned and stepped out into the hallway. She walked softly down to stand beside the door to her parents' bedroom, afraid to knock. What if she said something and it only made things worse? Everything she'd done so far had only made a mess of things. Penelope stood by the closed door, willing her father to appear.

He didn't come.

Where is he? she wondered

He didn't come and he didn't come.

Penelope put a hand on the glass doorknob of her parents' bedroom, but she couldn't bring herself to turn it. How could *she* possibly help her mother? She had made her mother cry. She had done enough already.

Or *had* she?

What, exactly, *had* she done?

Penelope thought for a minute about the wishing well. She let go of the doorknob.

She stepped away from the door, chewing her lip, deep in thought.

Then Penelope realized something. *Wait!* she thought. *If the well is magic, and this is my fault, then I can fix it. And if I can't fix it—it isn't my fault at all!*

Straightaway she ran downstairs, grabbed a pencil and a sheet of paper from the kitchen table, and dashed out into the garden, where she stood by the well. *This might not work,* she told herself, *but it can't make things any worse.* With a brief thought for how best to word her wish, Penelope bent over and scribbled a note.

> I just wish something would happen to make everything better right away!

Then she crumpled the sheet of paper, shut her eyes, and whispered into the wad of paper, "I know this is crazy, but *please please please?*" She kissed the wad of paper and tossed it into the well. Without even peering after it, she turned and ran back inside, to see . . .

But when Penelope got inside, nothing was better at all. Delia was still crying loudly enough to be heard throughout the main floor of the house, and Dirk was still missing.

Deeply disappointed, Penelope trudged down the hallway toward the stairs. She felt worse with each step. The well hadn't worked. Her father was off in a bathrobe somewhere, muttering. Her mother was sobbing. Sobbing! Mothers weren't supposed to sob, were they? It occurred to Penelope that she didn't actually know anyone else's mother. *Maybe mothers do cry,* she thought. She pushed the thought from her mind. It wouldn't help. Nothing would.

Suddenly—the doorbell rang.

Dong! went the deep chime just as Penelope entered the foyer. She paused.

Upstairs the crying stopped as if by magic.

Dong! The bell rang again, deep and sonorous.

Penelope turned nervously to face the door.

Dong! It rang a third time.

The deep sound echoed through the downstairs as Penelope flew toward the door. Although she wasn't supposed to open it when her parents weren't in the room, she didn't even think twice about that today. Something was *happening.* She knew it. She could feel it.

As the bell rang out a fourth time, Penelope pulled on the heavy oak door and opened it just a crack.

"Hello?" she asked bravely.

"Telegram!" called out the boy on the other side of the

door. He was a freckled kind of boy, almost a grown-up. He wore a funny red uniform and stood beside a silver bicycle.

"Really?" asked Penelope curiously, swinging the door open the rest of the way. She didn't know what she'd been expecting, but it wasn't a telegram.

When the boy caught sight of the foyer, with its gilded picture frames full of long-dead Greys, its antique carved chairs, and its inlaid marble floor, he whistled low and raised his eyebrows. "Whoa!" he said. "*Excellent* house! I've never been in one of these big old places before. You guys must have a blast here!"

Penelope tilted her head and thought about that. She was not sure what he meant by a *blast*, but she was fairly certain it didn't describe the time they'd been having. "Not really," she said.

"Well," said the boy. "That's too bad for you, I guess."

"I guess it is," said Penelope honestly.

The boy didn't seem to know how to respond to that. "O-okay then," he said. "So, here you go! Telegram for Delia Dewberry!" He held out a bright yellow envelope.

"Oh!" Penelope looked at the envelope. "Dewberry? You want my mother, I think. Though she can't come down right now, and anyway, she hasn't been Delia Dewberry for years and years. She's Delia Grey now."

"That's cool," said the boy.

"Who sends a telegram?" asked Penelope. "I've never seen one before."

The boy gave a funny little grin. He had very large teeth. "Generally an old person from somewhere far away," he said. "I just need your signature right here, please?" He held out a clipboard. "You can sign for your mom."

Penelope had never signed for anything before, and she smiled as she reached for the pen. Even with all the terribleness around her, she enjoyed the feeling of holding the clipboard. She gave her name an extra curlicue or two, then handed the pen and clipboard back to the boy.

"Thank you," she said, taking the envelope and beginning to close the door.

"Wait—aren't you going to open it?" asked the boy, pushing back against the door. "I'd love to know what it says." He looked very eager.

"Why?" asked Penelope.

"Well, because nobody sends an unimportant or boring telegram these days. Anyone who goes to the trouble of sending a telegram has something interesting to say. Plenty of easier ways to tell people regular things— what with e-mail and cell phones and text messages and everything. If someone goes to the trouble of sending a telegram, it's almost always worth hearing about."

"But the telegram isn't for *you*," said Penelope.

"So what?" asked the boy. "*My* business isn't especially interesting, so I like to know other people's too. Don't *you* ever snoop? Look through your dad's sock drawer? Listen at doors?"

Penelope remembered lurking behind the French doors on the day of the *everything change,* but she wasn't going to tell some stranger about that. She shook her head. "Not really."

"Oh," said the boy. "Well, you could start now!" He grinned even bigger and eyed the envelope in an obvious way.

Penelope frowned at him slightly. When she realized she was making a Delia face, Penelope crossed her arms and tapped her foot too. It was a funny feeling. For just a second she almost *felt* like Delia.

"Ah, well, you can't blame a guy for trying," said the boy.

"Why not?" asked Penelope, uncrossing her arms. But just as she spoke, the sobbing upstairs started back up. A loud wail made its way down the staircase and through the open door. Penelope cringed.

The telegram boy raised an eyebrow. "I hope the

news is good. News sometimes is, and it *does* sound like someone could use some cheering up. Have a nice day!"

With that, he tipped his hat and climbed on his bike. Then he rode off down the stone steps of the mansion. Penelope gasped as he bumped down the stairs and landed safely on the sidewalk.

4

A Little Big News

After she'd closed the door, Penelope stood in the cool foyer and quickly examined the object in her hands. Besides being a cheerful yellow, it appeared to be a normal enough envelope, made of thick paper. In its top left corner, in a funny old-fashioned font, the envelope read:

Donsky & Donsky, Esqs.
4811 Main Street
Thrush Junction,

Delia's sobs began to subside again as Penelope tried to make out the , but the envelope had gotten badly smudged. She wondered why there was no zip code and puzzled over where Thrush Junction might be and who her mother might know there. She turned the envelope over and noticed it was already mostly open. A pale piece of paper was winking at her. There was writing on it, and . . .

Could she? Did she dare?

Penelope held her breath, and with a fingernail she slit the flap of the enve-  lope the rest of the way open. She peeked over her shoulder and glanced up the stairs, but her father was nowhere to be seen. Slowly, she began to slide the piece of paper out and—

A particularly awful sob filtered down from above. Penelope's heart lurched. A long wail followed. Elsewhere in the house a door slammed shut and feet began to shuffle from somewhere to somewhere else.

Penelope slid the paper back into the envelope and raced up the stairs, her heart beating fast. With one hand she gripped the envelope, while she slid the other up the rich burnished wood of the banister. When she got to her mother's door, she steeled herself for what she might find on the other side, and knocked lightly. It was funny how the envelope in her hand felt like a reason to enter, a ticket of sorts. "Mother?" she called out. "Hello?"

The weeping stopped. "Yes?" came a breathy voice from the other side of the door.

"Can I . . . come in?" asked Penelope.

For a moment there was silence. Then, "Yes, dear," called her mother weakly. "Of course. Come in."

Penelope turned the knob and peeked into the room. She cleared her throat. "There's a telegram," she said, holding the envelope out to her mother like a gift, with the open flap down. "A telegram came for you. Here."

Delia lay in her big bed, looking very small. She wiped away her tears and replied, "A *telegram?* Really?"

"Yes," said Penelope. "For Delia *Dewberry*. It's yellow. It looks important. I didn't read it. It was already open," she said guiltily. "Mostly." Her mother didn't seem to care much about that.

Delia sat up and gathered a thick blue blanket around herself comfortingly.

"Who on earth would be sending a telegram?" Delia said with a sniffle. "I think the last time I saw one of these I was twelve!" She took the envelope and ran her hand over the thick paper with a fond smile. "My grampy sent me one every year on my birthday."

"That's nice," said Penelope quickly. Under normal circumstances she'd have been happy to hear stories about Delia's grampy, but right now she only wanted to know what the telegram said. She hoped that her mother would be distracted by its contents, but also, she was just plain curious.

Delia gave a little chuckle now, remembering. "My mother had a silly song she'd sing as I opened it each year—*Big shazam, thank you ma'am, happy birthday telegram!* I'd forgotten all about that. How funny!"

Penelope smiled. It had been a while since she'd heard her mother sing anything.

Delia looked closely at the envelope for the first time and read the return address. As Penelope watched, Delia's eyes went wide, and her throat caught. She whispered to herself, "Well! Would you look at that—Thrush Junction!"

"Where's *that*?" asked Penelope.

Dirk chose that very moment to bumble into the room, coffee cup in hand. He noticed Delia's tear-streaked face and leaned over and kissed the top of her head. "Sweetheart! You look like you've been crying. What could be the matter?"

Penelope thought this was a ridiculous question, and she found her father's timing terrible. Couldn't he have picked *any* other moment in the last few weeks—or even the last half hour—to pay attention?

Delia smiled weakly and kissed Dirk's cheek. "I'll be fine, dear. I've just had a lot on my mind lately. Things we should talk about later. But look!" She held up the envelope brightly.

"Hey, what's that you've got there?" he asked.

"It's a *telegram*," said Penelope impatiently. "Addressed to Delia *Dewberry*. Open it, Mother, please!"

"I am, dear. I am." Delia lifted the flap of the envelope and carefully extracted a piece of paper, which she read to herself.

Penelope stood anxiously on her toes. She could tell from the way her mother's eyes were moving up and down the page that she was reading its contents more than once, but from the astonished look on her mother's face, Penelope couldn't make out whether the news was very good or very bad. She waited, full of tingles.

At last Delia looked up and set down the telegram.

Dirk put down his coffee cup and sat on the bed beside his wife.

"What?" cried Penelope. "What?"

"Yes, *what?*" asked Dirk in much the same tone. He bounced slightly up and down on the bed. "Read it aloud, darling!"

So Delia cleared her throat and read these words:

Miss Dewberry stop

Please forgive delay stop We write to
inform you that your great-great-aunt
Elsbeth Lenhard Dewberry has passed
away stop The property known as the
Whippoorwillows (106 Merry Widow Lane)
is yours stop Please arrive before
August 31 or forfeit property, by terms
of will stop

Congratulations stop
Tolly Donsky stop
DONSKY AND DONSKY ESQS stop

PS: Most sincere condolences stop Betty
was a special lady stop

"Great-great-aunt?" asked Penelope.

"Yes. Betty," said Delia. "She was my grampy's aunt, I think, though I never met her. Gosh, I can't believe she's been alive all this time and I didn't know. We didn't really keep in touch with that part of the family, and my parents always made her sound like a batty old bird, but it would have been nice if I'd known she was there, especially after Mom and Dad died." Delia sighed and set the note back in her lap.

"A house! You've inherited a *house?*" asked Dirk. "Where *is* this house?"

"A house!" echoed Penelope in wonder.

"Thrush Junction," said Delia. "East Tennessee." Then she looked at Penelope wonderingly and said, "In the country, dear, probably quite a rambling house. Just like you were wishing for. Isn't that funny!"

It *was.*

"East Tennessee?" said Dirk. "I don't know much about Tennessee. There are mountains there, right?"

Delia nodded. "It's not just *a* house. It's the Whip-poorwillows. Thrush Junction." She sighed, with a funny, faraway look in her eyes. "My grampy used to talk about this place. He spent summers there when he was a boy, and he always made it sound—magical."

Magical? The hairs on Penelope's arms suddenly stood on end.

Delia tucked a strand of hair behind her ear and sat up straight. "I guess I need to make some phone calls. I'm not sure what I'm supposed to do next, never having inherited a house before."

"Well," said Dirk in a knowing way, "you might not want to fuss around too much with it. You might think about putting the place straight on the market. Summer is the best season for real estate."

"Sell it?" asked Delia, looking confused.

Penelope's heart thumped. "No!" she cried.

Dirk shrugged. "I'm just saying, Tennessee is a long way away. Plus, the money might come in handy."

"Yes, money *might* come in handy." Delia frowned at her husband. She glanced around at the piles of laundry and dirty coffee cups on the bedside table. "Dirk," said Delia, "I think we need to talk. I fear there are some things you don't understand about our—erm—current situation."

"Sure, of course," said Dirk, scratching his stubble of a beard and pondering the situation. "Though maybe we shouldn't sell after all. I suppose we could keep it to use as a summer house or something. Could be kind of nice. Do you think it has a veranda? Southern houses often have verandas."

Delia cleared her throat and stared meaningfully at

Penelope. "Dirk, I mean we should talk *alone*. Right now. About *money*."

Dirk looked over at his daughter. "Ah, I see what you mean. In that case, perhaps Penelope might run down and fetch me—oh, I don't know—how about some juice? I'm absolutely parched." He raised his eyebrows at Penelope.

"What a nice idea," Delia chimed in with a pert nod. "Penelope, please fetch your father some juice."

Penelope headed out the door grumbling. She remembered what the telegram boy had said about snooping and made certain to leave the door cracked behind her. As she started down to the kitchen, she overheard her mother saying, "About the money, Dirk—I don't think you understand—"

At that, Penelope stopped grumbling and ran the rest of the way down. *It would be nice to be able to talk out loud about everything,* she thought. Maybe they could even open some more doors.

Behind her the voices faded, and Penelope dashed into the kitchen, where the only juice left in the fridge was some overly thick prune juice of a questionable vintage. She dripped it into a small glass and snuck back upstairs as quietly as she could.

When she reached the top of the stairs, she heard her mother saying, "But, Dirk, it's my family land, and it says we'll forfeit the property if we don't come down ourselves by August thirty-first. I think that's what we have to do."

Penelope charged into the room, nearly spilling the prune juice. "We're moving to the country?" she cried, excited. This was *exactly* the kind of thing that happened in books.

Dirk dismissed Penelope's outburst with a shake of the head. "Of course we aren't *moving* there, Penelope," he said. "Your mother was merely suggesting a visit before we sell the place, *maybe.*" He looked over at his wife curiously. "Though if, as your mother has also just suggested, we can't afford Josie or a visit to the beach, I don't see how we have the money for *this.*"

Penelope's face fell. "Oh," she said. "I thought—"

But Delia was staring at Penelope now, almost *through* her. She stood up suddenly and said, "Why *not*, Dirk?"

"Why not what?" asked Dirk.

"Why *not* move there?"

Dirk looked exasperated. "I thought you just *said* we can't afford two houses!"

"We can't," Delia said. "Let's sell *this* one."

"What?" cried Dirk. "You want to leave The City and move to Tennessee? Sell the house I grew up in? Are you *serious?*"

"Maybe," said Delia with a nod. "It sounds crazy,

I know, but this could be a fresh start. A chance to begin again, to begin *better*. A place we can actually afford, even now. I wouldn't have thought to suggest it. It seems wild, and unlikely, but Penelope's idea isn't really so far-fetched, if you consider what our life has been like the last few weeks, and what we could sell this place for! Why, we could pay off all the credit cards and make a little nest egg. Then we'd have money to live on, and you'd have all the time in the world to write." Delia looked elated.

Penelope glanced from one parent to the other. She crossed her fingers and held her breath.

Dirk, on the other hand, looked downright shocked. "My family's house? We *love* this house! We're the envy of everyone we know."

"Yes," said Delia a little sadly. "It's a marvelous house, and I know it was important to your parents, but maintaining it costs far more than we can afford. Besides, we don't really *need* it, do we? Half these rooms never get used."

Penelope squeezed her crossed fingers tighter. She could feel her face turning red.

"Even so," said Dirk, "we have a great life here, don't we? Do you really want to move to the country? Won't it be boring?"

Penelope let out her breath silently but kept her fingers securely crossed.

Delia put a hand on Dirk's shoulder and said gently but firmly, "Maybe it will, but, Dirk, let's be realistic. We can't afford to stay here anymore. We're in the hole. Whether we move to Thrush Junction or not, everything will need to change. Even if we stay in The City, we'll need to move sooner or later, to an apartment, in a cheaper neighborhood. However unexpected, *this* is a solution. *This* is an answer. *This* is fate. Like a wish come true, a dream I didn't even know I had until this very minute."

Penelope stared at her mother.

"But what will we *do* there?" Dirk responded. "It's considerably away, and I'm no kind of farmer."

"Write books?" said Delia simply. "Go hiking? Get regular jobs? Start over? Buy ourselves a little time to figure things out?" Delia's voice sounded serious, but it had none of the sad, strained tone Penelope had been hearing for weeks.

Dirk stroked his unshaven chin again and shook his head. "I don't know," he said, but he said it slowly, as though he were now considering the idea.

Penelope crossed her arms behind her back, in case her fingers needed a little help. She crossed her legs too.

"Penelope?" said Delia, noticing. "Do you maybe need to use the ladies' room?"

Penelope shook her head and uncrossed her legs, but inside her tennis shoes she attempted to cross her toes. Then she glanced up at her father, who was still stroking his stubble.

"How about this," said Delia. "How about we try to *rent* this house out, to begin with? Would that make you feel better?"

"I don't know," said Dirk. "It all sounds crazy to me."

Delia paused for a moment, then said, "As crazy as quitting your job on a moment's notice?"

Penelope gasped.

"Hey! That's not fair," protested Dirk. "I was going *bonkers.*"

"So am I," said Delia simply.

"Me too," whispered Penelope. She didn't mean to. It just slipped out. "Sorry," she added.

Dirk looked down at Penelope, and then over at his wife, as though seeing them both in a new way. "Is it really that bad?" he asked. "*That* bad?"

Penelope bit her lip and said nothing, but Delia nodded solemnly. "I don't think about anything else, Dirk. I never minded being poor before I met you, but being in

debt and trying to live like we're rich when we aren't—
it's horrible! *Please?*"

Penelope waited anxiously, with her tightly crossed
fingers beginning to hurt a little. She watched her father
think. Dirk looked from his wife to his daughter several
times. He closed his eyes. Then, suddenly, he opened his
eyes, slapped his hands together, and smiled mischie-
vously. "Well," he said. "I guess it's time to pack our
camels! Look out, world! The Greys are moving to the
country!"

"Really?" Penelope cried.

Delia beamed and threw her arms around her husband's neck in a way that Penelope had never seen her
do before. Dirk and Delia kissed loudly, which made
Penelope weirdly happy, but uncomfortable at the same
time.

"You know," added Delia once she'd untangled her
arms from her husband's bathrobe sleeves, "I *do* like
the sound of this. Whatever happens, it's sure to be an
adventure."

BOOK TWO

※

CONSIDERABLY AWAY

5

OUT OF THE SHADOWS OF THE CLOUDS

Penelope watched in awe as the house began to wake up around her.

Overnight Delia stopped avoiding bill collectors and chewing her nails. Instead, she spent her days packing boxes and printing out maps. She sold most of their furniture for great wads of folded bills, and then (with a huge sigh of relief) took the wads to the various places where she owed money around town. Delia paid Josie her back wages and found a real estate agent to work on renting out the mansion. She also traded in the shiny black car Freddie had driven for a used van. It was a hideous clunker the color of dried mustard, but Penelope liked it. Her mother named it Dijon, which seemed just right.

While Delia was readying for the move, Dirk woke up, got dressed, put away his box of papers, and surprised Penelope by taking complete charge of the housekeeping.

She'd hardly ever seen her father lift a finger around the house before.

Of course, the place wasn't quite as tidy as it had been under Josie's watchful eye, but slowly the doors began to open again. The lights came on and the house was no longer a pit of despair. In fact, Penelope thought her father actually seemed to enjoy sweeping the porch, dusting the shelves, and making lunch. It was funny, how he'd stand back, mop in hand, admiring a particularly clean floor, and say proudly, "Now, would you just *look* at that shine! *That's* a job well done. Nobody could expect a man to do better."

Penelope packed her own room, carefully fitting her

books into boxes and labeling them. She also helped her parents, wrapping up glasses in newspaper and lemon-oiling the furniture to be sold. Each night as the Greys sat in the kitchen together, eating pizza or Chinese takeout and laughing, Penelope found she was happy, and a little proud too.

Whether or not her well-wishing had played a part in this strange turn of events, it had been Penelope who'd answered the door and signed for the telegram, and Penelope who'd first suggested they move to Thrush Junction. As things got better and better, she felt good about whatever it was she'd done to help.

Still, it was all a little baffling. "Do you *like* being poor?" she asked her mother one afternoon, seated on a box in the library eating a peanut butter sandwich while Delia packed up books.

Delia answered slowly. "I don't know," she said. "But I'm beginning to think that maybe I didn't especially care about being rich."

It took a few weeks for them to get ready, but finally the house was packed and Dijon was loaded. They all climbed into the van, buckled their seat belts, and— pulling a trailer with a few pieces of furniture, some suit-cases, and several boxes of books behind them—headed off into the unknown. As they crossed a big bridge and

lope thought no meal could rival their picnic
of bread and cheese and sliced tomatoes and
n the tiny porch outside their room. The Greys
astic lawn chairs, and Penelope smiled in the
ellow light of the porch. She listened to buggy
rick and cheep and chirp. She stared at the vine
ate purple blossoms growing up the drainpipe
er. "What's that called?" she asked her parents,
at the vine.

hat bougainvillea? I think that's bougainvillea!"
k, popping an olive into his mouth.

, dear," Delia said gently. "That's wisteria. I'm al-
tain."

ne thing, pretty much, right?" said Dirk.

steria," mouthed Penelope, memorizing the un-
name. Starting tomorrow, there would be a lot of
ngs and places and names to remember.

next morning the Greys were eager to be on the
in, but they were also ravenous, so they stopped
d hearty breakfast in the first town they found.
t down at their table in a place called Momma's
Land, in clean clothes, with their hair still wet.
dering omelets and toast and juice and coffee (for
Delia), the Greys found things slightly less perfect.
, there was a hair in Delia's water glass. Then the

left The City in their dust, Delia rolled down her window
and sang out, "*Take me hooooooome, country rooooooads!*"

Penelope smiled in the backseat, wedged between a
box fan and a garment bag. She'd never heard her
mother sing quite so *out loud* before, but it made her feel
like singing too.

Dirk drove, smiling and telling the occasional joke.

Penelope was in charge of the map. She followed with
her finger, tracing their slow progress along the tiny lines
that cut across rivers and lakes, mountains and state
lines. Whenever she looked out the window, she found
herself mesmerized. First by the wide highway and all the
other people, the strangers on the road beside them.
Kids in cars picking their noses, and truckers smoking
cigarettes. Then she stared at mountains: blue mountains
in the distance and green mountains up close, low and
lush and filled with small creeks and rickety bridges. The
big highway gave way to a smaller highway, which in
turn gave way to a winding two-lane road that cut deep
into the hollers and hills.

Funny, thought Penelope, *that once you're in the mountains, you can't see the mountains. I guess maybe things look
different when you're part of them.* She noticed that some
of the mountains had dark places on them. Large spots
that were a heavy green color, almost black.

"Why do they look like that, with some spots that are darker than the rest?" she asked her parents, straining against her seat belt to lean forward into the gap between the front seats.

"I think those are shadows," her dad said without taking his eyes off the road.

"Shadows of what?" asked Penelope.

"The shadows of the clouds," said Dirk. "They're there all the time, but you can only see them in the mountains or on big open plains. Isn't it pretty?"

It was pretty, though Penelope found it strange to think that she'd been living her whole life under shadows she hadn't known were there.

The Greys stopped occasionally for bathroom breaks, and twice so that a deer could finish crossing the road. Once, they parked at a small produce stand by the highway, where they bought the reddest tomatoes in the world and ate the most delicious peach pie any of them had ever tasted.

Penelope couldn't help being a little jittery about moving to a strange new place at the age of (nearly) ten— a place where she knew nobody and nobody knew her, and where she'd probably be different from everyone else—but she also felt tingly at the thought of the adventures that lay ahead. Thrush Junction would be full

of new people, new friends. T
thought, *a real school full of kid*
and excitedly, what *that* migh
by and Penelope had nothing
could only do for so long in t
felt ooshy), she stared at the
around her and grew more an

Just after dusk the Greys
called the Alpine Lodge. Penel
from the drive, but she had ne
before, and she thought the p
Greys' room was sweet and ol
palest pink. The white sheets
small vase of wild roses sat on
window of the room, and the
were shaped like roses too.

Penelope explored the roo
stood in the sliding-door closet
the little refrigerator, where h
stowed the food from their coole
bed (where she found a lucky per
desk by mistake when she pick
leafed through a pile of tired pap
and changed channels on the TV
lying on the little cot on wheels,

Pe
dinne
olives
sat in
blurry
thing:
of de
besid
point
"
said I
"
most
"
"
fami
new
T
road
for a
The
Hap
Afte
Dirk

coffee was cold. Once Agnes (the cranky waitress) had brought hot coffee, they discovered that the cream in the tiny metal pitcher was clumpy. After that, Dirk stuck his elbow in a smear of grape jelly, and Delia discovered a broken toilet in the ladies' room. Finally, there was an awful, but appropriate, grand finale to a terrible meal: when the food arrived (after nearly an hour), Agnes managed to slide Penelope's cheese omelet right off the plate and through the air, into her lap.

"Oh no!" said Penelope, stunned, looking down at her lapful of eggs.

"Sorry, kid," said Agnes in a voice that sounded anything but sorry. She reached into Penelope's lap and simply flopped the crescent of eggs back onto the plate with a none-too-clean hand. "I hate when that happens." Then she dropped the plate in front of Penelope and walked back over to the cash register.

Dirk and Delia looked at Penelope in horror. Penelope stared at the eggs on her plate and then at the now-greasy lap of her favorite blue shorts. With a tiny paper napkin she attempted to wipe off the spot of grease. It only smeared into a bigger spot.

"We'll get you a new breakfast right away," said Delia efficiently, glancing over at the surly waitress and beginning to raise her hand.

"No." Penelope shook her head. She tapped the eggs with the tines of a slightly dirty fork. "No," she said. "No, these eggs are fine."

"What?" said her mother. "Why on earth—"

"Really," said Penelope. To prove it, she shoved a bite into her mouth as her parents stared. "They're *fine*," she said through the eggs.

As silly as Penelope knew this sounded, she needed for it to be true. The eggs *had* to be fine. Penelope had escaped from boredom and sadness and silence, and now she wanted *everything* to be good and fun and happy. She didn't want to jinx the move by making things unpleasant now. She didn't want to complain. The eggs would be fine if Penelope said they were fine.

Her father looked at her as though he seriously doubted the fineness of her lap eggs. "Don't be silly, Penelope," he said.

Penelope tried to convince him with a quick nod and another bite. "I mean it—they're yummy. See?" As her parents continued to stare in disbelief, she shoveled the eggs into her mouth and nearly choked on a lump of congealed cheese.

Penelope wanted to get out of Momma's Happy Land as quickly as possible. If they could just get away from this greasy place, things could go back to being perfect. She ate faster.

Penelope was still chewing grimly when Agnes headed over with the check and asked in a perfunctory, waitressy way, "Everything okay here, folks?"

"I *guess* so," said Dirk with a doubtful look at his daughter. "We're about done anyway."

Delia just nodded stiffly, the way people do at the end of a meal that is not worth complaining about. "Fine, fine. I *suppose.*"

Penelope nodded too, with a grim smile and a mouthful of eggs.

But just as Dirk was reaching into his billfold and Agnes was tapping a toe to hurry him along, Penelope gagged on a bit of toast crust. She reached for her juice to wash it down, but when she drained the glass, she found herself staring at a bug. A big black fly, drowned and stuck to the bottom of her glass.

Penelope couldn't help it. She retched.

Agnes asked again, "Everything okay, kid?"

Penelope retched again, and suddenly things weren't okay at all. Looking at the fly, Penelope wasn't afraid of jinxing anything anymore. She was too disgusted to care! "No," she said, setting down her glass with a bang. "No, it's *not.*"

"What's that, Penelope?" asked Dirk, handing Agnes some money. "Everything all right over there?"

Penelope shook her head. "No. Everything is *not* all right. It is—*was*—awful. I don't mean to be rude, but the eggs were cold, and I almost drank a fly just now." She held up the glass for everyone to see.

Instantly, Penelope felt better. *Actually*, she thought, *it feels good to complain.* It was a little like stretching.

Agnes stared at Penelope, her mouth hanging open slightly. After some thought she said, "A fly, huh? Sorry, kid."

"You know," Dirk said to Penelope, "there are lots of nutrients in flies. Maybe we should be glad they don't charge us extra. Right, Agnes?" He looked up at the waitress, who said nothing in reply.

Delia gave Dirk a light thwack on his shoulder. "Dirk!" To Agnes she said, "I'm terribly sorry for my husband's bad joke." Her lips twitched as she added, "He's been a little addled since he joined the ranks of the unwashed unemployed. Please forgive him."

Agnes shrugged, shook her head, and shuffled off, back to her spot at the register to fold napkins.

"Ugh," Dirk whispered at Penelope across the table. "Really, that was the *worst* coffee I've ever tasted. Like engine oil. If there's such a thing as *weak* engine oil."

Penelope smiled.

"And those eggs!" hissed Dirk. "Tough as tire tread.

Were they even eggs? *Dinosaur* eggs, maybe!" Dirk screwed up his eyes, stuck out his tongue, and said, "Blech!"

Penelope giggled.

But Delia—Delia *snorted*!

Penelope blinked in surprise. She had never heard such a sound come out of her mother's mouth. She stared at Delia, who was covering her mouth with a hand, her eyes wide. Delia snorted again!

Then Penelope began laughing out loud, and she couldn't stop.

In a minute all three Greys were laughing at nothing, and everything.

They deserted their booth, still giggling and snorting and laughing. Grinning at each other, they fled the diner and walked speedily away from Momma's Happy Land.

Happy.

"That was fun," Dirk whispered to Penelope as the door swung shut behind them with a sigh.

Penelope had to agree.

Back in the car, filled with a terrible breakfast but a deep appreciation for her parents, Penelope drifted off to sleep, lulled by the hum of the road and the green forever of the trees and the tranquil hills outside her window. Worn out from all the excitement and the travel, she slept a long time.

The next thing she knew, she was being roused by her mother's voice calling out brightly, "This is it! Main Street, USA. Rise and shine, darling!"

6

WELCOME TO THRUSH JUNCTION

Penelope stared out the window. *This* was Thrush Junction, her new home, the answer to her prayers? This was hardly even a town. Whatever she'd imagined, she hadn't imagined *this*. She remembered what her father had said about things being boring. Where *was* everyone?

In the late-afternoon sun the van moved slowly past a line of little shops that sat on a small hill—old-looking shops, just a few blocks of them, with wooden storefronts covered in peeling paint and saddled with sagging porches. The scrabbly yards were overgrown, and the sidewalks were cracked. On a few of the porches people sat, waving slowly as the Greys drove past.

LIVE BAIT AND TAXES, read the sign on one store.

A restaurant proudly proclaimed SOUP!!! WE GOT IT! *With three exclamation points*, Penelope thought, *it must be extremely good soup.*

They passed a storefront that said JACQUELINE SANCHEZ, MD: SPECIALIZING IN FINE WHINES SINCE 1984.

Dirk chuckled. "Well, they've got a sense of humor here, anyway."

At the very top of the hill was a very old, very fancy, very official-looking building with a spire on top and a big bell. The entire structure was covered in some kind of bright green vine.

"What's *that* place?" asked Penelope, peering up at the overgrown building.

"The sign says that's the town hall. Also the mayor's house, the police station, the firehouse, and the courthouse." Delia squinted, reading the small print. "In a really small town, I guess everything is multipurpose. To make room for everything, and everyone."

"And what's that?" Penelope pointed to another building, a square, sort of ugly industrial building made of yellow brick. Painted on the side of the building were enormous red and purple letters that said WAKE UP, KIDS!

"A suggestion?" suggested Delia.

Penelope turned around to stare behind her at the funny square building. When she did, she noticed another, smaller sign that read THRUSH JUNCTION ELEMENTARY/ MIDDLE. Penelope started to feel a little worried. It didn't look like the kind of small-town schoolhouse she'd read about in books. It barely had any windows!

Delia began to slow down as they passed a few houses, and then turned onto the narrowest, windiest dirt road Penelope had ever seen. There was no sidewalk, just green everywhere. The road was flanked by trees whose branches touched in the middle of the road, forming a verdant archway overhead covered in small white blossoms.

Penelope took little note of the lovely trees because she was distracted by a girl walking up the road toward them. The girl looked about Penelope's age. She wore a faded blue dress and a pair of bright red high-top tennis shoes. She was also carrying what appeared to be a dead possum. The girl was swinging the possum by its tail as though it were no big deal at all. As the Greys passed her in their car, the girl smiled and waved her free hand.

Penelope ducked down in her seat. Despite the girl's friendly smile, she felt suddenly numb. What had she wished upon herself? Did she even have any idea what living in the country would be like? Did she really want to live here? Could she make a place for herself among the peeling paint and dead possums? She wanted a change, she did, and yet—

Penelope wondered if maybe her old life hadn't really been so bad. Even if she'd been bored, at least she'd had her beautiful house, and if Jane and Olivia hadn't been especially exciting, at least they hadn't played with dead things.

Penelope gave a shiver that was partly about the possum and partly about the sudden realization that she'd have to *make* friends before she could *have* friends. She'd have to get to know a pack of strangers who all knew each other, who'd grown up together and were very different from Penelope. Maybe her clothes were all wrong. Maybe *everyone* played with dead animals. When the Penderwicks had gone to the country, they'd had each other, but Penelope was all alone. Making friends wasn't something she knew very much about, except what she'd learned from books. Maybe it would be awful here, where everything was so new and strange. For the first time in Penelope's life, she felt like she might need a sister, or even a brother. Too bad. Not much she could do about that.

Turning around to peer through Dijon's back window at the girl they'd just passed, Penelope gulped. The girl was off in the distance, but Penelope could still make out

the possum swinging beside the girl's long braid of reddish hair.

Penelope was so preoccupied with staring behind her that she barely noticed when Dijon pulled off onto a little gravel drive and ground to a halt in front of a very strange house. Quickly, she flipped back around in her seat to look out her own window.

"Here we are," said Delia, turning off the car.

They all stared.

"Is this ours?" Penelope asked. "The whole thing? *All* of them?"

Dirk looked perplexed. "It's a very *numerous* kind of a house," he said.

What they were all staring at was the fact that the Whippoorwillows—if that was what they were looking

at—didn't really look like a house. It looked like much more than that.

The main structure was a stately brick house that had seen better days, a tall red rectangle with peeling white trim, a grand old porch that wrapped around the building, and a set of stairs that ran up the right side of the house to the second floor. The house sat in a pleasantly sunny spot at the end of the tree-canopied gravel drive, surrounded by a clump of weeping willow trees. But that was just the beginning, because on either side of the main house were several other houses, tacked on to each other. *Cottages*, thought Penelope.

There were two of these connected cottages on the left side of the main house—one white and one purple. There were three on the right—in hues of orange, pink, and red. The only thing all the cottages had in common was that they looked homemade, lopsided, different. They were slightly different sizes and shapes. Some were covered in wooden clapboard, and others in shingles. The red house on the far right end actually appeared to have been made out of old doors. Running between the little front yards of the houses were tiny picket fences. In the yard of the white house, a hand-painted wooden sign read GOOD FENCES MAKE GOOD NEIGHBORS. The overall effect was that of a mother hen, flanked by her chicks, waiting to cross the road.

Penelope scrambled out of the van and stared. Six houses! She wondered if she could have a whole cottage to herself for a playhouse. She liked the purple one best of all.

Penelope felt the gravel crunching beneath the rubber soles of her shoes. It was a new feeling, unfamiliar but pleasant. She looked at the cracked porch steps and the peeling paint of the main house, and for some reason, she thought again of the girl with the possum. When she did, she felt a twinge of alarm.

But staring up into the green of the willows and down the winding dirt road, Penelope also felt a thrill. Gazing at the mountains beyond the house, she wanted to ramble, to *do*—in a hungry, wandering, *real* way. Looking at all the tiny cottages, Penelope wanted to explore. She had never felt so excited, or so nervous. Penelope had never felt so *much*.

"Wow," Dirk said to Delia, opening his door and stepping out of the van beside Penelope. "Our new family estate is . . . um . . . interesting. If a little dilapidated."

Delia climbed out too and walked around Dijon to join the others. "Yes, it's *different*," she said, breathing deeply and listening to the birds in the trees above her. "But it's *ours*, and we can afford to keep it. Why, once we find someone to rent out the house in The City, we'll have more than enough to pay for our groceries and keep the lights on while you write your book! Maybe we can even rent out these extra little houses as a bed-and-breakfast. That would be fun! Besides, my grandfather said that it was the most special place in the world when *he* was a boy."

"That might have been the last time they replaced the roof on this place," laughed Dirk. "But sure, why not? I'm game for adventure."

He popped open the trunk and reached in for his messy box of papers and a few shoulder bags. "No reason to sit and stare. Might as well open up the house. I wonder how long it's been since your aunt died." He walked across the gravel drive and stomped up the rickety steps as though testing them.

Penelope and her mother followed more carefully behind him, and they were all facing the front door of the big brick house when it suddenly flew open.

The Greys jumped!

But there was nothing to be scared of. The person standing before them was only a girl, a girl about Penelope's age. She had a tangled mess of jet-black hair, enormous brown eyes, skin the color of wet sand, cutoff jeans, and filthy feet that Penelope couldn't help noticing. She had to wonder where *those* feet had been.

"Hullo!" the girl said. "What took you so long?"

The Greys stared at the girl in shock.

The girl looked patiently amused.

Penelope waited for one of her parents to say something. Neither spoke.

At last the girl laughed and shook out her curls. "Take a picture. It'll last longer!"

This woke Dirk from his momentary trance. "Hey!" he said. "That's not very polite."

"Neither is staring," said the girl with a shrug.

Penelope was impressed. This girl was like the house itself, a little wild and a little scruffy and a little scary and a little wonderful.

"Hi," Penelope said softly. She held out a hand awkwardly. "Hi. I'm Penelope. What's your name?"

"Luella!" said Luella, staring at Penelope's hand, which dangled in midair, unsure of itself. After a moment Luella wrinkled her nose and added, "Your name is *Penelope? Really? Penelope?* You don't look like a Penelope at *all*! You look like a Kate. Or maybe an Annie. If I were you, I'd change it."

Penelope didn't know what to say to that. She withdrew her hand quickly and put it in her pocket. She felt her mother's arm come around her protectively.

"That's very rude, Luella," said Delia, shocked. "Penelope Grey is a *wonderful* name. It's perfect, and I don't know why you'd want to hurt my daughter's feelings."

Perfect? thought Penelope. Maybe it *was* a nice name, or a pretty name even, but Luella wasn't wrong—*Penelope* had never felt like a perfect fit. Of course, she couldn't say that to her mother.

"I didn't mean any harm," explained Luella. "It's a *fine* name for *someone*. It just isn't right for a kid like *her*." She jerked a thumb at Penelope. "But that's just *my* opinion. I didn't mean to hurt anyone's feelings. Really." She stared at Penelope, eyes wide open, as though she was waiting for something. For all her bluntness, it seemed as if she really was sorry.

"It's—okay," said Penelope cautiously, staring back

at Luella, and then, looking up at her mom, she attempted a smile. "Really, Mother. I'm fine." And she was.

Luella rewarded her with a wide grin. "Oh, good! I'd hate to upset you on your first day. I do that sometimes, upset people. Without meaning to."

"I suppose . . . ," Delia said carefully. "I suppose we'll let it pass. It's—um—nice to meet you, Luella. But, if you don't mind my asking, what are you doing here?"

"Well," said Luella, "right this minute I'm talking to you."

Penelope stifled a giggle.

Delia found Luella's answer less clever. "Hmmm. It would seem you are. Does your mother know where you are?" She reached out to push an unruly curl from in front of Luella's eyes.

Luella laughed as the curl sprang right back. "*That* never works! And yeah, of course she does! Mom'll be home later if you want to talk to her."

Now Delia looked completely puzzled. "What do you mean by *home*? Isn't this the Whippoorwillows?"

"Sure is," said Luella. "And that's *home*."

"It is?" asked Delia.

"Well, they'd hardly let me live here by myself," said Luella. "I'm only ten, after all." She darted a look at Penelope, a look that asked, *Is your mom nuts?* Penelope smiled and shrugged ever so slightly, but inside she warmed.

Penelope wanted to tell the girl that *she* was about to be ten too, but for some reason she was having trouble opening her mouth. It appeared to be stuck.

"Hey!" said Dirk, heading for the front door of the house. "I have an idea. Perhaps we can take this rather confusing conversation inside. My arms are getting tired, and it's hot. What do you all say? Come on!"

Dirk began to walk past Luella, but as he reached for the screen door at the front of the house, Luella said, "Oh, did you guys want to come over to *our* place? I thought you'd want to go to your own apartment first." She pointed to the porch roof above their heads. "Mom said to give you the key." With her other hand she pulled a single key from her pocket, a key on a length of twine.

"Apartment?" asked Dirk. He looked upward. "What *apartment?*"

Luella sighed in an exasperated, impatient way. "*Are* you or *aren't* you moving into Up-Betty's place?" she asked.

To Penelope the girl whispered, "She *died* in there, you know!"

"Up-Betty?" Delia looked bewildered. "Do you mean my great-great-aunt Betty? She lived in an *apartment?*"

Luella nodded.

Delia ran a hand through her hair and said, "But I thought I'd inherited the *house*. I'm very confused."

"Look," said Luella. "I'm just a kid. All *I* know is that Up-Betty died, and Mom said you were taking over her place and that I should give you this key when you got here." She held up the key. "And I hope you plan to do that, because it's spooky having a big empty apartment up there. There are creaks all night long. *Someone* needs to move in up there to scare off the ghosts."

"Ghosts, huh?" said Dirk. "I wonder—is there an *adult* we could talk to, maybe?" He reached for the key.

"There's Old Joe in the white house," said Luella, waving vaguely toward the cottage at the end. "I *guess* he's an adult. But he's about a hundred and two, and kind of *past* being an adult. It *is* the middle of the day, you know. Most people are at work."

"How about this," Delia said, turning to Dirk. "Why don't we just put our bags in the upstairs apartment for now, and then drive into town for an early dinner? While we're there we can find Donsky and Donsky, Esquires. I'm sure *they* can explain all of this."

"Sounds fine to me," said Dirk. "I'm starving. Though I didn't see much in the way of fine dining downtown."

Luella, her eyes fixed firmly on Penelope, piped up.

"*You* might like the fried chicken at the Junction Lunch."

"Thanks," said Penelope, whose mouth appeared to be working at last. "I love fried chicken. It's my favorite." (Which was true at that very minute, though it never had been before.)

Luella smiled brightly and added, "Hey! Mine too! I wonder what else we have in common."

Penelope stared at her feet happily. All things considered, this was going well.

As they all trooped up the stairs to the second floor of the main house, Penelope whispered to Luella, "Don't tell my mom, but I think you're right about my name. Penelope Grey sounds like someone who wears a fox fur with a face."

"Exactly!" said Luella loudly. Then she confided, "If you want to know the truth, *I* changed *my* name when I was five. There were already too many Emilys in my kindergarten class. Me, an *Emily*!" Then Luella turned and stomped down the stairs.

7

Settling and Unsettling

The first thing Penelope noticed about the apartment, after setting down her little suitcase in the big open living room beyond the door, was that it felt like a tree house. High up and full of windows, it looked out onto a sea of green willow trees and out over the thick lush landscape and the mountains beyond. But this was no ordinary tree house! It was a tree house furnished with faded Persian carpets and Chinese screens, leather ottomans and dusty copper tables, Navaho beaded slippers hung on doorknobs, and huge Greek-looking statues serving as coatracks. And everywhere—covering every wall—were posters and pictures from places all over the world, in languages Penelope couldn't even identify.

The Chinese screens were cracked and the carpets were threadbare, the leather was dried and the copper was tarnished, but none of that mattered in the least. It was the most interesting place Penelope had ever seen. She moved slowly around the big open living room, examining and touching each object. She was so absorbed that she barely registered her mother's voice a few feet away, bemoaning each crack, each chip, the missing crystals in a chandelier. Penelope's fingers grazed every surface, and she wondered how on earth all of these things had gotten here.

After a while Delia and Dirk moved on to another room, and Penelope found herself sitting on the floor beside a wooden crate. The side of the crate was stamped with the word PEACHES, but inside it were stacks of magazines and pamphlets so old that they crumbled at Penelope's touch. Still, she couldn't resist them. Gingerly she pulled a pile from the crate and laid them in her lap for a closer look.  They weren't just old, they were ancient! *Black Bess,* one was called. *Varney the Vampire,* read another. According to the dates on each magazine, they were more than a century old! This place was almost like a museum.

Penelope opened one up as gently as possible. When she did, she found that it was nearly unreadable, eaten by moths and mice and many years. *That's too bad,* she thought, closing the magazine again to gaze at the picture on the front.

Just then Dirk came back into the room. "What have we here?" he asked, crouching down beside Penelope and peering over her shoulder.

"Just some magazines I found," said Penelope. "They're neat. They're old."

"Well, would you look at that!" exclaimed Dirk. "Real honest-to-gosh penny dreadfuls! I've never actually seen one before."

"Penny dreadfuls?" asked Penelope.

"Sure," said Dirk. "That's what you call magazines like this. They're, like, the very first comic books. Cheap old action stories. Chock-full of excitement and mystery. Thrills on every page, though not exactly what you'd call great literature. But they're neat, aren't they?"

Penelope looked at the crumbling magazine in her lap and thought about that. *Full of excitement and mystery* sounded awfully nice to her. "They really are," she said.

Dirk stood up again. "Too bad these are in such bad shape. Or they might be worth a *pretty penny*. Ha! Get it?"

Penelope groaned at the terrible joke. Then she set the magazines back in the crate and stood up herself, brushing the bits of crumbled paper from her lap.

"Penny," she murmured, liking the word on her tongue. "*Penny*," she repeated. "I wonder—"

"Wonder what, kiddo?" asked Dirk.

"I wonder if I could be Penny from now on, instead of Penelope. Like a nickname. Do you think Mother would mind?"

Dirk thought about this a second before he said, "You know, I don't see why not. We've got a new start here, a new town, a new life. Might as well try on a new name, eh?"

Penny nodded happily.

"Heck, maybe I'll change my name too—to Varney!" He bared his teeth and hissed at Penny.

Penny laughed. "Don't be silly, Daddy."

Then she mouthed the name to herself, testing it out. "Penny," she said. "Penny, Penny, Penny." She turned to Dirk and waved. "Hey there, my name's *Penny*. Nice to meet you!"

"Well, hello there, Penny!" said Dirk, waving back.

Penny laughed. The name felt easy. It was light and fun and cheerful and—right.

Then her father shot her a concerned glance. "Say," he added, "you aren't doing this just because that Luella girl made you feel bad about being a Penelope, are you? I'd hate to think that. It's a perfectly fine name, you know—"

"No," said Penelope, who was already feeling rather

like a Penny. "No, she gave me the idea, but really—I *want* to do this. I really do."

"In that case, I think it's a fine idea, *Penny*." Dirk whispered with a wink, "To tell you the truth, *I* wanted to name you Harold. Shows what *I* know."

Penny giggled and rolled her eyes.

"Now what?" she asked her father.

"I don't know, Penny," said Dirk. "I guess we go inform your mother of this big decision, and then hopefully we can *eat* something. Fried chicken sounds great right about now, don't you think?"

Penny did.

"Then let's see if we can pry your mother out of the linen closet. Delia!" he called, striding from the room.

A few minutes later the Greys were all piling into Dijon and heading back down the gravel drive and out to the winding road, in search of nourishment.

Luckily, the fried chicken at the Junction Lunch was every bit as good as Luella had said it would be. Better still, they soon discovered that in a town the size of Thrush Junction, a café waitress can be a very reliable source of family history, local lore, gossip, and community goings-on. The Greys were licking their greasy fingers and gorging themselves when their friendly waitress pulled up a chair and joined them for lunch.

"I'm Kay!" she said, setting down her own sandwich. "And since we're the only ones here, I thought I'd be neighborly and join you for lunch." She took a big slurp of her soda. "What brings you folks through Thrush Junction? We don't see many tourists, if you want to know the truth."

"Oh, we're not tourists," said Delia. "We're—new. We've inherited an old house here and—"

"Well, I'll *be*," said Kay, smacking the table joyfully. "You must be the new Dewberry folks! I'm so glad to meet you. I was friends with your aunt Betty."

Delia smiled hesitantly. "Yes—yes. I guess that *is* who we are. The *Dewberry folks*. Only we aren't called Dewberry. I'm Delia Grey, and this is my husband, Dirk. . . ."

Dirk waved a chicken leg in the air. His mouth was full.

"And who're you?" Kay asked Penelope directly.

"I'm Penny," said Penny, smiling a little nervously. "Penny Grey." Delia seemed barely to notice.

"So glad you're here," said Kay. "Truly a delight. How're you all settling in?"

"Well," said Delia, "we're a little baffled, if you want to know the truth. We thought we were inheriting a house, but the house seems to be full of people already. It's rather an odd situation."

"Oh, *that!*" laughed Kay. "Let me give you the skinny."

So while the Greys finished their lunch, the waitress explained matter-of-factly that while Delia had indeed inherited the house, she had also inherited a number of tenants.

"Tenants?" asked Delia.

"Well, maybe *tenants* isn't quite the right word," considered Kay. "Usually tenants pay rent. Right?"

"I think that's the way it works," said Dirk through a mouthful of homemade cinnamon applesauce. "Why wouldn't these people pay rent?"

Kay laughed. "Well, see," she said, "Old Betty—your aunt—"

"Great-great-aunt," sighed Delia, "though I never met her."

"Crying shame," said Kay. "She was a neat old gal. Always in the middle of everything here in Thrush Junction. She was a mover and a shaker, Betty was. Always busy. She ran off to see the world when she was a young thing, before I was born. But in her later years she was more of a homebody. Town mayor when I was small. Then she raised llamas, but she never had kids. Said she liked borrowing them from other people, but liked returning them even better."

Dirk laughed.

"That was fine, of course," continued Kay. "Only, while she was gone on her adventures, the rest of the Dewberry clan moved away, off to other parts. Betty got really lonely after your uncle Fred died, with no other kin to speak of. She just rattled around in that big house, talking to herself and her llamas. Eventually she invited Betty Jones to move to town and into her basement apartment. They'd been friends long before, years back."

"That's a charitable thing to do," said Delia, nodding in an understanding way, "to take in an old friend."

"Not sure Betty saw it as a particularly charitable thing," Kay said. "I think she'd have called it friendship, plain and simple. Not to mention that Down-Betty more than earned her keep, working the garden and helping with the meals. But even after that your aunt was still lonely, so she invited the Gulsons—Abigail and Rich, and later on they had Beatrice and Luella—to take over the first floor. She moved into the upstairs and gave them the bigger space. Said they needed room for a studio. They both paint, the Gulsons. Art when they can, and houses when they have to. Interesting folks. You'll like having them as neighbors, though Rich is away right now, I think. Working on some kind of a big mural somewhere. One of them *always* seems to be out of town!

Being an artist isn't as easy as you might imagine. But Luella is almost always around."

"Yes, we met Luella," said Delia.

"Spirited gal," added Kay with a wink.

"*I'll* say," said Dirk.

"So *then* what happened?" asked Penny.

"Oh, not much. Betty was finally satisfied. She liked it well enough, having them all there, but she was running out of room. Then, after a few years, Down-Betty Jones moved out of the basement and built herself the Grape Shed—that's what she calls her little purple house—and that gave your aunt an idea.

"From then on she just offered a place to anyone who wanted to come live with her—said they could build on like Down-Betty had done. And people came and gave her company for all her various schemes and adventures—her treasure hunting and her llama raising and her beer brewing."

"Treasure hunting?" asked Penny with interest.

"Beer brewing?" asked Dirk in much the same tone.

Kay didn't seem to have heard either of them. "For the last decade or so all these different sorts of folks have just come and gone as they've needed to and helped out in whatever way they could, bartering work for a place to stay. Which is often how things work here in Thrush

Junction. People do what they can and share what they have."

"That's nice," said Delia, "and yet—"

"Yet now *you've* inherited the house, because I guess you're Betty's next of kin, or last, but you've also inherited her friends!" said Kay. "She wrote up her will that way, and rewrote the deed to the house, from what I heard tell. That she was leaving the house to kin, keeping the Whippoorwillows in the clan. But all her housemates would get to stay on until they decided to leave, or died. Rent-free. Some said she was a little crazy in the end, obsessed with dusty old stories and caves and the like."

Penny's ears perked up at the mention of stories. *What kind of stories?* she wondered.

"But one thing you can say about Betty, she was good to her friends," said Kay, standing up.

"Well, that's very kind of her, but what am *I* supposed to do with all of these people," asked Delia, perplexed, "if it's in the deed that they get to stay?"

"I guess you could start by saying hello," Kay suggested.

That evening the Greys hauled their boxes into the upstairs apartment that was already so very full of furniture and art and knickknacks. As Penny watched her parents unpacking the box of wires and gadgets that went with their computers, she frowned. She couldn't help thinking they looked all wrong in the room. They looked too new, too businesslike beside the wonderful collage of Betty's unusual belongings.

"Mother?" she said as she watched Delia attempt to plug her laptop into the only phone jack in the house, which happened to be in the center of the living room, beside the fireplace. "That looks all wrong. It just doesn't—fit with Betty's stuff. It's too shiny."

"Well, what on earth can we do about it?" Delia asked. She set her laptop on the mantel, next to a painting of an old stone wall in what looked to be the Irish countryside. "We can't just get rid of everything Betty left behind right this minute. It would take a month to clear this place out, and probably there are people we should give these things to, her friends and neighbors."

Getting rid of *Betty's* belongings hadn't been what Penny intended at all, but it turned out not to matter because Dirk interrupted with, "Well, once we have the whole house to ourselves, we'll look into sorting it all out and setting up a real computer room, but for now let's just live with it all. Okay?"

Penny thought of Luella. She wasn't sure she wanted the tenants to leave, but she nodded at her father as she flopped onto an old wine-colored velvet sofa that smelled of dust and cinnamon. From there she watched her parents run around and make sense of their belongings, arranging and rearranging. Eventually Penny fell asleep. It had been a long day.

When she woke up, Penny sat up at once. She was in a room full of morning sunshine filtering through the willow-filled windows. Someone had moved her in the night, and she was puzzled at first by the unfamiliar room. Though she'd stuck her head briefly into every room in the apartment the day before, there had been too much to take in. She hadn't really noticed the blue rag rugs and the white iron bedstead. She hadn't noticed the ceiling, which was made of a bronzy-colored metal, covered in interesting patterns and designs. She hadn't seen the bookshelves in the corner, made of white wicker. Beside the bed she was tucked into were the boxes she'd packed in The City. Penny bounced gently and found that the bed beneath her was creaky but cozy. She sat in her covers and inhaled deeply the dusty perfume of dried flowers, lavender maybe. It was nice, like something out of *Little Women*.

Penny climbed down from her bed and poked around a little. She gazed out her new window, then headed into the living room. Her parents were already up, sitting on the couch munching toast and drinking their morning

coffee. Her father handed her a banana and made a spot for her beside him.

"Would you like some juice, dear?" asked Delia, handing her a dusty glass that read 1962 WORLD'S FAIR. "Careful not to spill! There's no dining room, and your father's covered the kitchen table with boxes, so we're having a living room picnic this morning. How's that?"

Once they'd all eaten breakfast, Dirk removed himself to his new office. Penny followed him and watched him arrange his new desk, which was painted bright yellow and blue and was surrounded by bookshelves built out of more peach crates. She watched her father shuffle around with his box of papers, but when he began to set up his files, Penny lost interest.

She went in search of her mother and found Delia in the avocado-and-chrome kitchen. The two of them ended up organizing the shelves, alphabetizing (and sniffing) the spice jars and bottles in the cupboard and trying to imagine what each old-fashioned kitchen implement was for. By lunchtime they were happily scrubbing out the refrigerator.

For that one full blissful empty day, they went nowhere. It was like the Greys were living in a tiny bubble. They ate from their cooler, and room by room they cleaned all the dingy and dusty old furniture Betty had left behind. They beat out rugs and fluffed pillows. When it began to get dark, they climbed through the living room window and onto the roof of the porch to watch the sun go down over the trees. They sat quietly together, and Penny found she could not stop smiling, sandwiched between her parents, who seemed like new people to her. Maybe Thrush Junction *was* small, and maybe it *would* be a little quiet, but so far it was wonderful. It was nice, fitting everything into five small rooms. It was nice, cleaning the house. It was nice, sitting together on a porch and not saying a word.

The last thing Penny did before going to bed was sit down in her nightgown in front of her new bookshelf and run her finger over the spines of the dusty old books Betty had left behind. She thought about all the new things there might be to do in them. Then she climbed into bed and went to sleep.

The next morning, after a breakfast of stale wheat crackers and bruised apples washed down with water, Dirk realized they'd completely run out of coffee. This meant that someone would have to venture out. Once Dirk drove off to do just that, the bubble burst. Delia decided that now it was time to "figure things out."

"As soon as your father comes back with the van,"

she said to Penny, "why don't we go find those lawyers? I'll feel better once we have the legal stuff taken care of. It's unsettling, not really knowing what's going on. You'll come with me, won't you?" Delia asked Penny. "I could use some backup."

Although a visit to the law offices of Donsky & Donsky, Esqs., was hardly how Penny had hoped to spend her day, she agreed to go with her mother. It was nice to be asked.

About an hour later when Dirk got back to the house, his arms full of bags and his conversation full of stories about the old-fashioned grocery store called the Mountains Mercantile, he pronounced it a good idea too.

"That's perfect!" he said. "You two go along to town while I get all of this put away and figure out lunch. Look!" He held up a loaf of fresh bread, as proud as if he had baked it himself. "People make *everything* from scratch around here. I got some homemade pickles too!" He held up a clear glass jar with a funny lid. "Makes me think even *I* might be able to bake something."

So Delia and Penny left him to his bags and boxes and bottles and cans and jars and plans and dreams. They climbed into Dijon and set off.

It was easy enough for Delia to find the offices of Donsky & Donsky, Esqs. Not only had Kay the waitress waved them in the right general direction, but the elderly sisters were the only lawyers in Thrush Junction, and their office was in a small blue building with a very large sign that read DONSKY & DONSKY: SISTERS-IN-LAW. It was hard to miss.

Delia poked her head in the door and called out brightly, "Hello? I'm Delia Grey—um—Dewberry. Delia Dewberry Grey! And this is my daughter . . . Penny. I'm here to sign some papers!"

Immediately, she and Penny were beckoned inside by a stern-looking elderly woman in bifocals who introduced herself as Myra Donsky. Myra asked Delia to repeat her name and then handed over a stack of very official-looking papers.

"Nothing to it," Myra said. "Congratulations on the new house. Just have a seat and sign here, here, and here."

After Delia had quickly glanced over and signed the requisite forms, another old lady—this one with a warm smile and a purple ribbon bouncing on top of her drifts of white hair—entered the room. This lady carried a *second* stack of papers.

"Hi," she said in a cheery voice. "I'm Tolly! So nice to have you in town." She set down the pile of paperwork. "Congrats on the house! Now, here you go, darlin'."

Delia looked at the pile blankly. "*More* papers?"

Penny peered over her mom's shoulder.

Myra and Tolly Donsky nodded at her in unison, as though they'd been rehearsing for this moment.

"Oh," Delia said, picking up a pen to sign. "I guess these probably have something to do with the tenants? I was going to ask you about them anyway—"

"No, nothing to do with that," said Myra sternly. "These regard the loans."

"What loans?" asked Delia. She stopped in midscrawl and set down her pen.

Penny watched her mother closely.

"You see, dear," Tolly Donsky said, leaning forward confidentially, "your aunt Betty was an astounding lady, and a generous soul, but she wasn't exactly good with numbers. She was often forgetful about her taxes, and then, just a few years before she died, she borrowed some money against the house when the llamas all caught foot-and-mouth disease and needed special care."

"Special care?" asked Delia in a wobbly voice.

"Yes indeed." Tolly nodded. "Sick llamas need a lot of love, and medicine, and that debt still needs to be paid." She tapped the pile of papers. "You need to fill these out so we can get you set up for monthly payments. That is, unless you've hit the jackpot recently, or something like that."

Delia shook her head wordlessly.

Tolly laughed gaily. "I didn't think so. Though one never knows. Folks do win the lottery now and again, strike gold!"

Hearing this, Delia turned to Penny and said quickly, "Penny, dear, why don't you go out and enjoy the sunshine."

Penny stood. She wanted to refuse, wanted to say that she'd rather help. But she didn't want to make things any harder for her mother, so she headed meekly outside to sit in a patch of thistles that had sprouted in the cracked sidewalk. When at last the office door opened, Delia marched past Penny without saying a word.

All the way home Penny tried to watch her mother without being too obvious about it. Delia's lips were narrow. Her brow was creased as though she was thinking very hard. In the office she had looked scared. Now she looked angry.

Penny asked quietly, "Mother, will it be okay?"

Delia didn't answer.

When they got home, Dirk was sitting in the living room eating a pear. "How'd it go?" he called out cheerfully.

"Not *quite* as smoothly as expected," called Delia in a firm voice. She didn't even bother to set down her purse, just motioned for Dirk to follow her into their bedroom.

As they walked from the room, Dirk asked through a mouthful of pear, "What's up? Is it about the tenants?"

"The tenants are the least of our worries," Delia replied. Then she closed the door behind her.

Penny flinched at the sound it made shutting.

8

FINDING A FRIEND

Penny sighed and headed for the kitchen, where she made herself some lunch (cheese and crackers and carrot sticks). Then she spent an hour at the front window of their second-floor apartment listening to the squirrels scampering overhead, watching the willows wave in the breeze, and trying not to worry. Since there was no alternative that she could see, she waited patiently for her parents to emerge and explain.

After a bit Penny began to notice things happening out in the yard. She saw a window in one of the cottages (the white one at the end) open. She watched an extremely old man holding something that looked like a violin case teeter to a rusted car that looked as if it wouldn't go, but then it did. And then, *then* she saw a girl about her own age step from the bright orange cottage just below her window. Penny stood up and stuck her head through the window, trying to get a better look at the girl below her. It wasn't Luella. Who was it?

Whoever she was, she was the prettiest person Penny had ever seen. She had long, shining, straight blond hair pushed neatly back in a lavender headband *exactly* like the one Penny was now wearing. Penny touched her own headband and wondered if maybe it was a sign. The girl was carrying an armload of what looked like library books. Books! Maybe she was the friend of Penny's dreams: a Betsy to her Tacy.

The girl smiled at nothing in particular, and as she bent to pick a few flowers from her little garden, Penny felt a wonderful nervousness well up inside of her. This girl looked like a kindred spirit. Penny could just imagine the fun they'd have swapping books, doing their homework together, and everything, everything else. Maybe there would be secret sharing and midnight feasting. Penny was happy to have Luella downstairs, but *this* girl looked perfect.

The girl began to walk slowly away, along the drive and through the willows. Penny stood up. This was her chance! She took a deep breath and hurried to the door, ready to make a friend. She pattered down the stairs that ran along the side of the house down to the porch, and practiced her hello. She knew just how she'd do it. She'd call out, easily and warmly, "Hey there! Want to play?" as though it were no big deal, as though it were just something she said to kids all the time. Not something she had to think about at all.

By the time she stepped down onto the planked porch floor, the girl was on the far side of the gravel drive, heading for the road. Penny mouthed *too* gently, too nervously, "Hey. Hey there!" It was almost a whisper.

Of course nobody could have heard a timid whisper at that distance, and the girl didn't even turn around. Penny watched her shining blond head bobbing away. Why wouldn't her voice work? Why was this so hard? Clearly she needed practice.

Penny walked down a few steps, took a deep breath, and tried again, louder this time. "Hey there!" she called out.

This time the girl stopped in her tracks and glanced around her feet as though looking for something. Almost as though she had heard Penny and was thinking about answering.

Seeing this, Penny felt a little less invisible. She felt a strange rush inside her. It was as though she couldn't control herself. Her legs and throat took over, and she ran to the bottom of the steps and fairly hollered, "HEY THERE! YOU! WHAT'S YOUR NAME?"

This time the girl turned around, and her eyes met Penny's. But instead of answering Penny's call, the girl just knelt to pick up the daisy she'd dropped from her bouquet, then looked up again at Penny motionless on the porch. The girl blinked, as though waiting for something.

Penny waited too. It was the other girl's turn to say something.

The silence went on too long. Penny stared, until finally the girl gave a slight shrug and turned back around, continuing on her way. Penny couldn't believe what had just happened. She knew she didn't have much experience with making friends, but she hadn't done anything *wrong*, had she? What else could she do?

Penny tried one last time. In a sudden burst, she dashed headlong down the steps and yelled at the top of her lungs, from the bottom of her heart, "PLEASE COME AND PLAY WITH ME! PLEASE? PLEASE BE MY FRIEND?"

Then she clapped her hand to her mouth, mortified.

This time the girl didn't even turn around. She

ignored Penny completely, stepped off the drive, and disappeared around the bend of the windy road.

Penny stood alone at the bottom of the splintery stairs feeling ridiculous. She resolved that she would never, ever do anything like *that* again.

A door slammed behind her. She turned to face the stairs and found the tangle-haired Luella at the very top of them. Luella was holding open a screen door and wearing the same dirty shorts she'd been wearing the day before. She pointed a finger at Penny and squinted down the stairs. "What's all the commotion? Who're you talking to? Who do you want to be friends with?" asked Luella accusingly.

"Oh, um, nobody," answered Penny as she felt the flush drain from her face. She walked back up onto the porch, trying not to look directly at Luella as she passed her. "I was just remembering something from a movie I saw one time. I was just saying some lines from that movie. Rehearsing them. I'm—uh—going to be an actress when I grow up." She blushed as she spoke the lie.

"Really?" said Luella. "*Really?*"

Penny nodded and headed for the steps to the second-floor apartment.

"*Really?*" Luella turned to follow Penny with her eyes.

Penny nodded again, gulping. She could feel Luella's

eyes on her back, just like people always seemed to do in mystery novels. Standing on the third step to the upstairs apartment, she turned and met Luella's gaze. "Don't *you* ever do that?"

"No," said Luella, staring back. Then she smiled. "*I* don't, but then, I'm going to be an archaeologist. Either that or an airplane pilot. I haven't decided."

Penny didn't know how to respond to that, but Luella seemed like she meant to be nice. Her smile was friendly. So Penny smiled back down onto the porch.

"Where were you all day yesterday?" asked Luella. "I figured I'd see you around, but you've been hiding out."

Penny only shrugged. It seemed dumb to say she'd been hanging out with her parents organizing the spices.

"Don't have much to say, do you, Penelope?" asked Luella.

Penny shook her head. "I guess not," she said. Then she thought of something. "But—oh! Guess what! I'm not Penelope anymore. I changed my name."

"You *did?*" asked Luella. "That was quick! What'd you change it to?"

"Penny?" said Penny.

"Pennnnnny," said Luella slowly. "Huh. Yeah, that's a good name, all right. *Really* good."

Penny beamed.

"You know, Penny," said Luella, "*if* you're lonely, and *if* you want to, you can come watch my worm battle." She said this as though she were bestowing a great gift.

"I'm *not* lonely," said Penny, tensing up. "I'm fine. I told you—"

"Okay then," said Luella with a shrug. "Suit yourself." She turned to open her front door and prepared to head back inside.

Penny watched the screen door swing open. "Watch your *what?*" she asked.

"Worm battle," said Luella, pausing before stepping inside. "Just a little worm battle. It's pretty fun."

Penny, who had never heard of such a thing in her life, not even in a book, walked back down the three steps to the creaky porch. Considering the unfriendly shiny-haired girls and the worried parents Penny was dealing with today, *pretty fun* sounded pretty good.

She followed Luella through the door and into an empty white room. There she stood looking around, while her new friend disappeared down a hallway and returned carrying a large terrarium, which she set on the floor. Then Luella rang a little bell, leaned into the terrarium, and yelled at two very sluggish earthworms, "Are you ready to RUUUUUMBLE?"

Penny sat on the floor beside Luella, and they waited for something to happen. After about four minutes, when neither worm had so much as rolled over, Penny tapped Luella on the knee cautiously. In a whisper she asked, "Hey, Luella? What's supposed to happen?"

"Shhh!" said Luella accusingly. "I think they were *about* to do something. Now you scared them."

Penny almost laughed at this suggestion. These worms did not look like they were capable of being scared. They looked dead.

As though she might be thinking the very same thing, Luella rapped gently at the glass. "Get up and fight, Billy the Bruiser! Wake up and show him who's boss, Chainsaw Charley!"

Neither worm looked like it had any interest in complying with Luella's wishes.

Luella pouted and sat back on her heels. She turned to Penny and said, "Cross my heart and hope to die, last time it was a bloody mess. They were on fire. They ripped each other to shreds. . . ."

Penny stared at Luella. This was clearly an exaggeration and probably a complete lie. *I know she doesn't want to be an actress,* Penny thought, *but watching Luella is kind of like watching a movie or a play.*

Luella kept talking. "They were in *pieces,* and you

know what happens when worms get cut in half!" Luella grinned and rubbed her hands together wickedly.

Penny did not know, but before she could say a word, one of the worms flipped over onto its back with a half-hearted squirm.

"Ooh! See!" said Luella, pointing. "*Now* they're getting *crazy!*"

This was the most absurd thing Penny had ever heard. She tried to keep a straight face, but the worms were so sad and limp, and Luella's claim so ridiculous, that Penny burst out laughing instead. Once she began to laugh, she found she couldn't stop. She just pointed at the pathetic worm and said, "Yeah, c-c-c-crazy! That's just w-w-w-what they are!"

Luella looked like she was going to argue, but then she started laughing too, and once they were both going, neither could stop. The two girls held their sides and laughed and giggled and pointed at the worms through the glass for a good three minutes. They fell over, they laughed so hard.

Finally Penny calmed down. Wiping away a tear, she propped herself on one elbow and asked, "Hey, what *does* happen when worms get cut in half?"

Luella rolled over and looked at Penny, mystified. "Are you telling me you've never cut a worm in half?"

"Why would I want to do that?" asked Penny. She sat up.

"I don't know," said Luella with a shrug. "Kids just do. Same reason you'd burn a leaf with a magnifying glass or do a puppet show or build a fort or hunt for treasure or dress up your dog."

"Oh, I've done a puppet show!" said Penny with a nod.

Luella stared at her. "You mean you've never built a fort?" she asked. "Not *ever*? Not even a small one?"

Penny shrugged. She was only now becoming aware of all the things she'd never done. This wasn't the wispy, floaty, vague sense of absence she'd always had, but a concrete picture of forts and worms and—well, every-thing. Penny didn't know what to do, so she just looked at Luella and shrugged.

Luella understood. She jumped up and called out happily, "Then why are we wasting time with worms? Let's get these guys back to the garden. You have some serious catching up to do!" She grabbed the worms in one hand and Penny with the other and ran quickly back out onto the porch, down the steps, past the row of cottages, and around back to a very large garden.

Penny, dragging along behind Luella, was so excited to build a fort with Luella that she almost ran into her father, who was wearing a pink straw hat with a wide brim, weeding lettuce beside a very old lady in a pair of overalls. She stopped just before she barreled into him.

"Hi, Daddy," she said, shielding her eyes from the glaring sun. "I'm playing with Luella. And worms."

"What a coincidence! I'm playing with worms too!" Dirk held up a giant nightcrawler. "Also I'm talking to Down-Betty here. She has some great stories. Makes me rethink the direction of my novel. I might shift gears, work on something more pastoral, more American gothic. What do you think?"

Penny didn't have any opinion on the matter (and she was beginning to seriously doubt that her father would ever finish his book), but it didn't matter because just then the old lady interrupted Dirk and changed the subject. She winked at Penny and said, "Hello, dear! I don't believe I've had the pleasure of an introduction—"

"Oh!" said Dirk. "I'm sorry! Betty, this is my daughter, Penny." He smiled at Penny, and she smiled back. "Penny, this is Down-Betty. Betty Jones. Your great-aunt Betty's friend. She lives in the purple house. You remember, Kay mentioned her?"

Penny waved, and the old lady smiled and waved back.

Luella sprinkled the worms out into the bed of lettuce. She turned to leave and motioned for Penny to follow.

"Sorry to run," Luella said to Down-Betty, "but we've got important stuff to do."

"Sure, girls!" said Down-Betty. "Thanks for the worms." She shook a handful of something green at them cheerily and flung dirt everywhere. "Now that we're all friends, why don't you both come by my place later for dandelion salad!"

"Thanks but no thanks," replied Luella. "We don't eat weeds. Do we, Penny?"

As she followed her friend away from the garden, Penny couldn't help thinking that her father's presence in the garden must mean that he and her mother had finished with their private conversation. She wondered what had come of the closed-door meeting. She wondered, but not enough to miss out on fort building.

Penny trailed off after Luella to collect sticks and vines in the thick wooded jungle of overgrowth behind the house, which began where the garden ended. Then she spent several very satisfactory hours doing just as her new tangle-haired friend instructed her to do, chattering and laughing and listening and asking questions, and getting very dirty in the process. At the end of the day the two girls sat in a very fine fort under a willow tree. They contentedly ate an entire jar of oatmeal chocolate chip cookies Luella snuck from her kitchen.

As Penny reached absentmindedly for the last cookie, Luella grabbed it away and gave her a gentle push. "Hey! You have to share the last cookie if nobody calls dibs. It's a rule!"

Penny was taken aback. She didn't know about dibs, though she was almost sure she'd read about it in a book. Maybe it had been a Ramona book? She handed over the cookie and said softly, "Here. You can have it. I didn't know. I'm sorry."

Luella looked skeptical. "Why?" She examined the cookie closely, and then glanced back at Penny. "Did you spit on it or something?"

"No," replied Penny. "Just—you can have it. I don't want to fight."

"Wow," said Luella, biting into the cookie without another thought. "You're kind of a doormat."

Penny didn't know what to say to *that* at all. She didn't like to be called a doormat, and she hadn't enjoyed giving up a perfectly good cookie that should, by rights, have been at least half hers. Luella had eaten more than her fair share already. She watched Luella munch the cookie and felt quietly angry, or sad, or something.

Luella noticed. She pushed Penny gently again, handing over the last bite but saying, "You know, Penny, that's not playing fair, getting all mopey like that. You should just say what you want, or call me a name or something."

Penny considered this advice. "Why?" she asked. "What good will *that* do?"

"Well, it'll make you feel better. Probably."

Penny thought this over. It made sense. "Okay," she said. "I'll try. Here goes."

Luella nodded at Penny in an encouraging way. "Good luck," she said.

Penny screwed up her face, and when she opened her eyes, she yelled, "You're a—a—a meanie!" She smiled hopefully. "How was that?"

Luella nodded slowly. "That's *pretty* good, but only babies use words like *meanie*. Honestly, I might have laughed at you if you'd said that in a real fight. Try again."

Penny thought for a second before she called out stiffly, but more loudly this time, "You're ostentatious and didactic!"

"Wow, yeah. That's better," said Luella appreciatively. "Certainly not babyish, but what do *those* words mean?"

"I'm not really sure," Penny admitted. "I just hear my dad say them sometimes. But I know they aren't something you want to be."

"Well," offered Luella, "why don't you try one more time, in words I know."

"Okay," said Penny. She thought of how much better she'd felt after her outburst at Momma's Happy Land, screwed up her face, and took a deep, honest breath. Then, all in a rush, she yelled as loudly as she could, "Your clothes are dirty and so are your feet and I really think you need to comb your hair!"

This sentence felt interesting and forceful coming out of her, like a gust of wind. When she opened her eyes, she found that Luella looked hurt.

"What? What did I do wrong?" Penny asked.

"Well, since you were trying to call me names, I guess you didn't technically do anything *wrong*," said Luella, turning away. "You did a *great* job of hurting my feelings."

"Oh," said Penny. "Oh no." Luella was so blunt and so tough. It hadn't occurred to Penny that Luella *could* be hurt. Now Penny didn't know what to do.

"Am I really *that* bad?" asked Luella. "I don't understand what my hair has to do with the cookie. Or my feet." She inspected her dirty feet.

"I don't know," said Penny, feeling terrible. This being honest thing was so difficult! Luella had called her a doormat. What was the difference? "I don't think they do. I'm sorry. I didn't mean that to sound so bad. You just— well, *you* called *me* a doormat. And your clothes *are* kind of messy, and I just never had a friend like you before."

"A friend like what?" asked Luella, turning back around to stare at Penny. "Do you mean poor?" Luella's tone was defensive, but her eyes looked sad and her voice was quieter than usual.

Penny wished she could go back in time and take back those words. Oh, why had she opened her mouth? Really, Luella's clothes looked fine. Who said anything about money? Who even really cared about clothes, anyway? "I'm sorry," she said. "Really. That's not what I meant."

"It's okay," said Luella, picking at a string that hung down from her cutoff shorts and sounding like it wasn't okay at all. "You're right. I *am* a mess, I guess. And you have such nice things. And your mother smells like a department store. But you don't *have* to play with me. I don't *need* more friends. There are plenty of kids around here for me to be friends with. Alice and Duncan and—"

Penny panicked. What had she done? This had been the most fun day she'd ever had, with her first worm fight, and her first fort, and she was dirty and sweaty and it had felt great. Better than in any book, even.

"No!" she said. "I don't mean that at all. I really am sorry. I didn't mean it. You don't understand. When I say *a friend like you* I don't mean what you think. I just mean—I've never—*never* had a friend before, I don't think. Not *any* kind of friend. Not a real one." In one short afternoon she had done more with this tangle-haired, barefoot girl than she'd done in her whole life of being friends with Jane and Olivia. "Gosh, Luella. You're—you're my *best* friend!"

Luella slitted her eyes and grinned at Penny. "Oh yeah?" Her voice sounded louder again.

"Yeah," said Penny honestly.

"Yeah?" asked Luella again.

"Yeah!" said Penny firmly, meaning it.

"Well then. You know what *you* need?" Luella asked, making a fist.

"No," Penny said warily. "What's that?"

"You need a noogie!" shouted Luella, teaching her very quickly what that particular word meant.

"Yow!" yelped Penny. Then she laughed and sank to her knees in a fit of giggles.

BOOK THREE

TRANQUIL HILLS

9

MESSY GROWN-UP STUFF

That evening Penny got home at dusk, ready to burst with stories about Luella and Thrush Junction. When she stepped inside, she found the house full of a wonderful smell. "Mother! That smells *good*!" she said in a surprised voice, stepping into the kitchen.

But Delia was sitting at the table scribbling some numbers on a pad and punching angrily at a calculator. "Oh, I had nothing to do with it," she said with a dismissive wave of her hand. "That's all your father's handiwork. It turns out he can *cook*. Who knew?"

Dirk stood at the stove wearing an old apron and stirring a pot of soup. "It's not so much, really. Nothing fancy. I just threw a bunch of stuff in a pot. It mostly came from Betty's garden! *Our* garden. Why, we're practically living off the fat of the land here." He took a sip of the soup and added, "It *is* good, if I do say so myself. Makes me think I *might* be a pretty good cook if I gave it half a try!"

He ladled out a bowl of the soup for Penny. He set the bowl on a plate and set a slice of thick-cut bread and butter beside it. Then he handed the plate to Penny and waved a spoon in the air with a flourish before slipping it into the soup. "Your dinner, milady!" he said with a bow.

Penny thought it was nice that her father was so proud of his soup. She set down the plate, pulled out a chair, and sat down at the table. As she lifted her first sip of soup to her mouth, Delia looked up distractedly and said, "Penny, why don't you take that along into the living room and eat it there?"

"Why?" asked Penny. "I haven't seen you all day. I have things to tell you! I have a *friend*!"

"Yes, yes, that's nice," said Delia, not appearing to have heard Penny at all. "But your father and I have a few more grown-up things to discuss," she said, tapping the calculator.

Dirk rolled his eyes at Penny behind Delia's back, but he nodded and whispered to Penny, "Go on ahead, chickabiddy. We'll hear all about your day later."

With a frown Penny stood up from the table and lifted her plate carefully, trying not to slosh. Then she changed her mind and set it back down. She looked at her mother, crossed her arms, and said, "No."

"Pardon me?" said Delia, looking up from her numbers. "No *what?*"

"No, I *won't* go into the living room," said Penny. "I'm tired of being shut out of things all the time. I'm *not* leaving the room until you tell me what happened today with those lawyers. I have a right to know."

"Oh, darling," said Delia, sighing and pushing back her chair. "I'm sorry. But you really don't need to bother yourself with thinking about money. It's not pleasant to talk about."

"Yeah, Penny," said Dirk, munching a leftover celery stalk. "Plus, it's boring too."

Delia shot him a cross look.

"I don't care," said Penny with her chin in the air. "Even if it's boring, or unpleasant, I *still* want to know what's happening. You guys are *always* closing the door on me."

Delia shot Dirk a questioning glance, eyebrows raised.

"She's got a point," said Dirk.

"You don't have to tell me *everything*," said Penny. "But you could tell me *something*. I'm not stupid. I can understand."

"No," said Dirk, looking at Delia. "She's *not* stupid."

Delia sighed, turned her chair toward Penny, and relented. "Okay, okay. If you really want to know—"

Penny nodded firmly. "I do."

"The short version," said Delia, "is that we inherited this house, but with it we inherited a great deal of debt—ridiculous debt—that my aunt amassed caring for a herd of rare, sick llamas, who all died anyway. If you can believe that." Delia let out a frustrated sigh. "When Betty needed money, she borrowed from the bank, against the house, so now that *we* own the house, *we* are supposed to pay that money off. We are supposed to somehow pay them a huge amount every month, starting *next* month."

"Oh," said Penny.

"Which," said Delia, "we did not budget for when we left The City. And which we do not have, since the real estate agent hasn't managed to rent out the city house!"

"Oh," said Penny again.

"The *other* problem," added Delia, "is that we also inherited all of Betty's friends, so we don't have the option of selling *this* place, because anyone who might want to buy it would also have to take the tenants rent-free, by the terms of the deed." Delia sighed again. "Though, if the bank forecloses on *us*, the terms of the deed will be null and void. So the *bank* could turn everyone out, or charge whatever they like in rent. *That* hardly seems fair!"

Penny was trying to follow, but it all sounded very complicated.

"It's quite a situation," added Dirk with a sour smile. "Just the sort of thing someone might put in a novel. Ironic, eh?"

"But what will we do?" asked Penny.

Delia shrugged. "Tonight? Eat soup, I guess. Think it over. Crunch some numbers. Hope for a solution. Pinch pennies. Look for a job."

"Oh," said Penny one more time, since she didn't know what else to say. She waited for her parents to tell her that everything would be fine, but all she heard was the buzzing of a fly caught against the window screen.

Delia looked at Penny. "I'm sorry the news isn't happier, but do you feel better now that you know?" she asked.

Penny thought about the question and shook her head. "Not better, really. But different. I think maybe I'll go eat in the living room now. Thanks for telling me—I guess."

"You're welcome," said Delia. "*I guess.* Enjoy your dinner, dear. I still need to do this paperwork, and your dad has offered to tackle the dishes, but we'll come in to see you later. Maybe we can all play a hand of cards or something."

Only they didn't. Dirk and Delia stayed in the kitchen for hours. Eventually Penny crawled into her creaky bed and went to sleep without reading. She had other things to think about tonight: real things, worrisome things.

The next morning Penny woke up and headed into the kitchen as usual. At the sight of Penny's rumpled hair, Delia smiled apologetically. She made room at the table and shoved a pile of napkins on top of the calculator and the pad full of scribbled numbers. "I'm sorry I was so cranky and busy last night, dear."

"It's okay," said Penny.

"No, it's not," said Delia. "But I promise, your father and I are done talking about money. For now, at least. Raspberry jam? Or strawberry? Both look good."

"Both *are* good," said Dirk. "They came from a little stand over at the gas station. Where they also happen to sell antiques and bluegrass records."

"I don't know," said Penny. She still felt a little confused about the money matters from the night before, but since her parents both appeared to be feeling better, Penny decided to cheer up too. She grinned. "I'll have both!"

"Nice move," said Dirk, handing her two pieces of toast, thickly spread with jam. Then he poured her a glass of milk.

Delia made more toast while Dirk told Penny about

the various fruit trees he'd discovered on his walk in the garden. Finally Delia cleared her throat and patted Dirk's hand. She said, "That's fascinating about the orchard, darling, but I think Penny said she'd made a friend. Wouldn't we rather hear about that?"

"Oh, yes, certainly!" said Dirk, pouring more cream into his coffee. "Do tell, Penny."

So, at *last*, with her mouth full of sticky jam and toasty crumbs, Penny had a chance to tell her parents about the day she'd spent with Luella, about the fort and the worms and the cookies. She even explained in detail what a noogie was, and generously offered to show them, though they declined. The whole time, her parents sipped their coffee and listened to her, looking quite happy despite their complicated woes.

"My grampy," Delia said at last, with a smile that looked a little wistful to Penny, "would be so glad to know you're here, running around like he did."

"Hey," said Dirk, "I bet you make even *more* friends today! I bet there's a whole slew of kids around here. You should just go knock on all the doors and say hello, introduce yourself, see who's around!"

Penny thought briefly about the girl with the shining blond hair and the flowers. She remembered standing at the bottom of the porch steps and blushed faintly at the memory. Then she thought of Luella and shook her head. "I only need one friend," she said. "One best friend."

Just then the doorbell rang. Penny jumped up and shouted out, "Hey! I bet that's her now!"

Delia smiled and reached for the newspaper as Dirk stood and headed for the sink full of soapy dishes.

But the person Penny found at the door did not look like her tangle-haired friend at all. *This* girl had her wild dark curls neatly pulled into two short pigtails. *This* girl had rolled the ends of a clean pair of cutoffs so that they looked like smart denim shorts. *This* girl was wearing a pair of blue sneakers tied with flowered laces.

"You look—different!" Penny couldn't hide her surprise.

Luella (because, of course, it *was* Luella, just cleaned up a bit) raised her hands to her little pigtails and gave them a twirl. "Eh, I figured I could try something new," she said. "Besides, it probably won't last long." As she said this, a curl escaped a pigtail and sproinged crazily to the top of her head.

Delia made a place for Luella at the table, and while Penny ate her toast and a yogurt, Luella drank a glass of juice and planned their day. Penny licked jam from her fingers and nodded at Luella's suggestion of a walk to

Main Street for penny candy. The two girls chattered as Delia read the paper and Dirk fussed about at the stove. It was all very pleasant until Luella began to read over Delia's shoulder.

"What're you looking for?" she asked, craning her neck to see what it was Delia had been reading. "Employment section, huh? You looking for a job? I heard my mom say the town needs a new garbageman. The last one *drank*." She made a tipping motion with her hand as though chugging a beer.

Delia folded the paper, saying, "Sometimes, dear, it's nice to respect other people's privacy."

"Oh," said Luella with a slight frown. "Sorry. I was only trying to be helpful, but if you're not interested, suit yourself." She turned away and took a loud sip of juice.

Penny glanced over at her friend and considered that perhaps Luella was still working on the being honest thing herself.

Dirk rinsed a plate and gave a chuckle.

"What's so funny, Daddy?" asked Penny, looking up.

"Nothing, really," said Dirk. "I was just trying to imagine your mother as a garbagelady."

Delia turned around and looked at him intently. "What's so funny about that?"

"Oh, well," said Dirk, registering surprise at her reaction. "I guess I just think of you as someone who likes pretty things. Nice smells and fresh flowers and good art. I just don't think of you as a garbage kind of girl."

Delia said nothing in response, but Penny noticed that the firm gaze she'd had at the law office had returned to her eyes.

"What kind of job *do* you want?" asked Luella. "What do you *do*?"

Dirk answered for her. "Delia here is good at all kinds of things, but when *I* met her, she was singing in a swanky nightclub in a long red gown. She was something else!" He whistled appreciatively.

"That's true," added Delia quietly. "And thank you, dear. But before I moved to The City and met you, I did all sorts of jobs. Some things even *you* don't know about, Dirk."

"Is that so?" asked Dirk. He looked surprised.

Delia nodded.

"Huh!" said Dirk. "Well, were you ever a garbagelady?"

"No," replied Delia thoughtfully. "No, I never was that. But I waited tables and gave piano lessons and worked at a pet store, and one summer I was a nanny to a family with *seven* kids. I've done *all* sorts of things."

Penny, who didn't even know her mom played piano,

was curious to hear more, but she was still in her pajamas, so she excused herself to get dressed.

When she got back to the kitchen, Dirk stood up. "Anyway, day's a-wasting. You girls want a ride anywhere?" he asked. "I need to run back to town. I want to see if I can find some saffron for this marinade recipe I found in Betty's old cookbook. It sounds interesting." He was holding his finger to a stained page in a dusty notebook.

"Nah," said Luella. "Walking is half the fun. Right, Penny?"

"Yeth," said Penny as she stuffed in her last mouthful of toast. As she swallowed, she couldn't help wondering how much her father *really* wanted to get back to his writing.

"Suit yourselves!" said Dirk, reaching for his keys.

Delia spread out the newspaper again and began to read.

"Are you ready?" Penny asked Luella.

"Always," said Luella.

10

BETTER SORRY THAN SAFE

Penny and Luella had just reached the porch when a terrible bellow began to sound. Penny gasped, but Luella didn't bat an eye. In fact, she didn't even seem to have noticed the noise. She merely continued picking orange juice pulp from her teeth.

"Luella!" cried Penny. "Listen! Should we get my dad?"

"No," said Luella, rolling her eyes. "That's just Mr. Weatherall, and it's almost certainly no big deal. But I guess we can go check it out. That way you can meet Duncan!" She took off in the direction of the little red house made of doors.

"Who's Mr. Weatherall?" asked Penny, running to keep up. "And who's Duncan?"

"You'll see," Luella called over her shoulder. "Come on!"

The screams continued as they ran. Just as they reached the door of the red house, everything went quiet.

"Oh!" said Penny. "I guess that means they're okay."

Luella made a face. "No. That just means Benadryl."

"What?" asked Penny. "Huh?"

"It's really nothing serious," said Luella, knocking on the door. "This happens about once a week. Duncan sneaks around and eats something that's on his list of allergy foods. When Mr. Weatherall catches him, he yells his face off. Then he stops yelling and gives him some Benadryl, just in case. It's kind of weird."

"*Kind of* weird?" Penny thought it sounded upsetting. "Mr. Weatherall is Duncan's dad?"

Luella nodded.

Just then the door swung open and a haggard-looking man peeked out, rubbing his chin worriedly. "Hello?" When he saw it was Luella, he pushed open the screen door. "Come in, come in. Maybe *you* can talk some sense into Duncan. He listens to you. I don't know what's gotten into that boy lately. He's been *eating* again."

"Yeah, I heard," said Luella, a hint of sarcasm in her voice.

"I just don't understand him!" fretted his father. "Why does he take such risks? Perhaps he needs to see another specialist. Do you think he has a problem?"

"I think *someone* might have a problem," said Luella, rolling her eyes at Mr. Weatherall, who was too over-wrought to notice.

Penny followed Luella, who made her way straight through the house. In the back bedroom they found a boy sitting on a bed. He looked like almost every other boy Penny had ever seen. He had brown hair and a few freckles, and he was wearing a striped shirt. Penny wondered why boys seemed to wear stripes all the time.

The average-looking boy was sipping a glass of water and frowning at the same time. Penny couldn't help noticing that the bed had guardrails on it, which seemed odd for a kid her own age.

Luella noticed too. "What's with the rails?" she asked.

"A new safety measure," groaned the boy. "In case I fall in the night. It was Mom's inspiration. She read some newspaper story about a kid who had night terrors."

Luella patted him on the back in sympathy. "Your dad said you've been eating again. What'd you get caught with this time?" she asked. "You big dummy."

"A grape," said the boy. "Man, oh man. This time he shook me so I'd spit it out. I hadn't even chewed it yet. It just flew right out of my mouth and hit his forehead!" He seemed a little proud of himself.

"Why do you *do* that?" asked Luella. "It only makes things worse. If you'd stop getting into trouble, they might actually let you come over and play more often."

"But if I stop getting into trouble, then I won't be doing *anything*," explained the boy. "I'll just be sitting here all sterilized, playing with educational toys and reading approved books, which are usually boring." He sighed deeply. "Getting into trouble is all I have. I just need to get better at being sneaky." Then he looked at Penny. "Hey! Who're you?"

All this time Penny had been standing back, taking in the situation and the conversation. Now she stepped forward and waved hesitantly.

"She's Penny, the new Dewberry," explained Luella. "She's a good egg." To Penny she said, "*That's* Duncan."

"Hi!" said the boy.

"Hi," said Penny. "I'm not *really* a Dewberry. But my mom is, kind of. My name's Penny. Why can't you eat grapes?"

Duncan sighed deeply. "It's on the list, so that means I *might* be allergic," he said. "That means it *might* kill me."

"Oh," said Penny, thinking that if that were the case, he should probably just listen to his parents. But all she said was, "That's terrible."

"It's no big deal," said Duncan. "*Really.*"

Penny was puzzled. "Really?" she asked. "Well, it *sounds* like a big deal."

"It's not, trust me," said Duncan.

"What's on the list besides grapes?" asked Penny. "What else *might* you be allergic to?"

"Just about everything," Duncan said. "I'm very fragile. You ought to see the pictures from when we went to the beach! I had to wear SPF seventy and a big dumb hat. Mom says I have very sensitive skin."

Duncan didn't look especially fragile or sensitive to Penny, no more so than anyone else she'd ever met. But looks could be deceiving. Maybe Duncan was like an upsetting book with an ordinary, happy cover. Maybe he was *Bridge to Terabithia*. "I've never heard of a grape allergy," she said.

"Yes," said Duncan. "It's very rare."

"A *lot* of the allergies Duncan *might* have are rare," said Luella with a roll of her eyes. "Apples and pears and oranges and sugar and salt. Plus all the usual suspects— milk and wheat and stuff like that!" She looked apologetically at Duncan. "Right, Dunc?"

"Yeah," said Duncan sorrowfully. "I pretty much live on rice and bananas. Oh, and boiled chicken, and of course my vitamin supplements. For a treat I get to have sno-cones sometimes. But they're *plain*-flavored."

"That's too bad," said Penny, who had never herself eaten a sno-cone. She had only seen other children walking down the street with them in The City, their faces stained red and blue and green and purple.

"It is," agreed Luella. "But to make matters worse, Duncan here is bad about breaking into the refrigerator— which they keep a weird super-childproof latch on—and he always seems to get caught. So he's also *always* in trouble. He's *always* grounded."

"Yeah," said Duncan. "*For my own good.* I'm a danger to myself!" He looked proud of that part.

Just then Mr. Weatherall appeared in the doorway. "Kids! You forgot to sanitize. Here you go!" He thrust a bottle of clear gel at Penny. "Be sure to clean *between* your fingers. You've been outside."

As Penny rubbed what smelled like floor cleaner onto her hands, Luella made a face. "Hey, Mr. Weatherall. Can Duncan come with us and play? We'll be extra careful and keep an eye out for him. I promise."

Mr. Weatherall shook his head. "No, he needs to stay home today and rest up after his ordeal. We wouldn't want him overexerting. Plus, you never know what might happen to him if he left the house, walking around in the *outside*. He might walk into a hornet's nest or something."

Penny, in her civilized life of sedate walks and supervised playdates, had never been one to get into trouble. But she'd also never been told she couldn't do things like take a walk. Suddenly she could imagine the appeal of troublemaking.

"Why would he walk into a hornet's nest?" she asked.

"Because he doesn't know better," said Mr. Weatherall. "He's never spent time outside. He isn't a tough cookie like you big rough girls. He doesn't know how to fend for himself. It's a dangerous place, this world of ours, and Duncan doesn't know how to do all the things you do."

Penny was delighted to be lumped into a category with Luella, but she knew that she wasn't terribly rough or tough, not really. Plus, Duncan was no smaller than she was. In fact, he looked like he had a good few inches on her.

"But how will he ever learn to avoid hornets if you don't let him go outside and get used to them?" she asked Mr. Weatherall.

"He WON'T!" cried Mr. Weatherall, causing Penny to take a step backward. "It's an *impossible* dilemma." With his head in his hands, the poor man dragged his weary self from the room. "Please be good, kids. I've just got to lie down for a minute. I need an aspirin." He shut the door behind him.

"Quick!" hissed Duncan the minute the door closed. "Now's my chance. He's gone!"

Before Penny could even ask what she was supposed to be quick about, Duncan was opening the window. Lickety-split (as though she'd done it before), Luella shoved a chair up under the doorknob to jam it. Before Penny could say "Huh?" Luella and Duncan had jumped through the window and into an azalea bush.

Penny had no choice but to follow behind. Never having crawled through a window before, she was a little clumsier than the others, and she scraped her knee on a drainpipe when she landed.

The three kids made straight for the fort beneath the willows and sat down on the ground, which was only a little damp with dew. "I bet we've got a good half hour before he comes to check on me," said Duncan. "A full thirty minutes of freedom. Ahhhhh!"

Penny was still trying to figure out the events of the last ten minutes. "I just don't understand," she said. "Why would you want to risk an allergic reaction? I certainly wouldn't."

Luella laughed and said to Duncan, "We'd better explain."

Duncan nodded. "Go right ahead."

Luella turned to Penny. "He's *not* allergic, or fragile either. His parents are just very, very nervous. Beyond nervous. Nutso. All the time. Both of them."

"It's the truth," agreed Duncan. "On account of the fact that I was born very early, and the doctors had to put me in an incubator and everything. They told my parents I might develop serious allergies and be smaller than the other kids. So now Mom and Dad think I *am* smaller, and that I *do* have allergies. It's ridiculous."

"Oh," said Penny. "That sounds hard."

"It's just plain silly, is what it is," said Luella. "Since really Duncan's fine."

"I totally am," said Duncan, nodding. "Or I *feel* fine, anyway. I can run and climb and do all the normal kid stuff. But all those years of being careful must have done something to my parents." He shook his head. "I'm not sure *they're* so fine. They're afraid of *everything*—absolutely *everything*. Mom is always doing research on the Internet about diseases hardly anybody ever gets. Dad only allows toys made of wood because he doesn't want me touching plastic. But I'm *ten*! I don't want a wooden sailboat, and wooden LEGOS are just plain crappy."

"Why no plastic?" asked Penny.

"Toxins," said Duncan wisely. "Plastic is just *full* of toxins."

"Poor guy," said Luella, patting her friend on the back. "He doesn't even get to go to Thrush Junction Elementary with us because of all the bad influences and the peanuts in other people's lunches. His dad is home-schooling him instead, which might be neat if it were *your* dad, or *my* dad, but—"

"But you've *met* my dad," cut in Duncan, rolling his eyes at the leafy branch ceiling of the fort.

At the memory of her own lonely days sitting with boring Joanna, Penny's heart went out to Duncan. "Oh," she said. "*Oh*, I see what you mean."

"If only there were a way to prove to them that I'm not so fragile," said Duncan with a frown.

"If only," added Luella, "you could shake them out of it. Show them that *you're* a tough cookie too. But how . . . ?"

Penny was quiet, thinking for a bit. Then she said, "I suppose—I *suppose* you could run off somewhere else and eat everything on the list all at once, in one sitting. Then they'd *have* to admit you're okay, right?"

Duncan and Luella stared at Penny in surprise.

"It's a good idea," said Duncan. "But I don't think it would work. They'd just give me Benadryl like always and then say how fortunate I was that they discovered me so quickly."

Penny pondered this. Then she said, "Don't *let* them discover you. You just have to *wait* to announce that you've done it. If you wait for a few hours and you're still okay—then your folks won't have any reason to give you medicine at all. It will be too late by then. You won't be dying, so they'll *have* to admit you aren't allergic."

"Say," said Duncan. "That's actually a pretty stupendous idea!"

Luella patted Penny on the back proudly and grinned a little wickedly. "I *told* you she was a good egg."

Penny glowed. "It's no big deal," she said.

Luella had a thought. "But what if you *are* allergic?" she asked. "I'd hate to lose you, buddy."

Duncan shook his head, decided on this matter. "I'm not," he said. "I just *know* I'm not. Look at all the things I've managed to sneak over the years. If I were really so allergic, *something* would have affected me by now."

"*Everything,* huh? That's a lot of food," said Luella. "I don't know if I could eat that much in one sitting."

"Oh, I could eat *anything,*" said Duncan, sounding confident. "I've been saving up room for years. But where will we get it?" he asked. "All the food, I mean?"

"My dad just went to the store," offered Penny.

"We've got soup and bread and jam, I know. But I don't think he got *everything*."

"They have *everything* at the Junction Lunch!" said Luella. "But it'll cost a lot. Do you have any money?"

"Not enough," said Duncan, pouting. "I spend my allowance on candy bars when kids come by the house selling for school fund-raisers. Then I hide them in my closet. Do you have any I can borrow?"

"I have six dollars and twelve cents," said Luella. "I was saving up to buy a skateboard. But you can have it. And we could go raid my mom's change jar. That's not *really* stealing. Maybe if we put all our money to-gether—"

"Oh!" said Penny, thinking of something and sitting up. "Wait! I have some money!"

For years Penny had been storing any change she found or was given in a piggy bank she'd had since she was a baby. It was pink and ugly and ceramic. Since Penny had never needed money or gone anywhere on her own, she'd never had any reason to break the bank and spend the money inside it.

"Hang on," she said as she sprinted off toward her apartment.

It took Penny a few minutes to find the bank in one of the unpacked boxes. Then she ran back, holding the bank under one arm and a video camera under the other, and trying not to drop either.

"Why the camera?" asked Duncan.

"For proof!" she replied, handing it to Luella. "If we record the whole thing, your parents will *have* to believe you!"

Duncan patted the shiny pink bank. "What's the pig's name?"

Penny stared at the ceramic pig in her arms, shining in the sun. "I never thought to give her one."

"Too late now," said Luella, who was eager to get

on with it. "Do you want me to do it?"

"No," said Penny. "I think I want to do it myself."

"Okay. Hop to it!" said Luella impatiently. "Smash it good!"

Penny let go of the pig, simply letting it fall from under her arm. It dropped meekly to the ground and rolled over.

"That," said Luella, "was pathetic. SMASH IT!"

Penny picked the pig back up and took a deep breath. She held it over her head, squeezed her eyes shut, and hurled the pig with all her might.

SMASH! went the pig, hitting a large rock.

Penny opened her eyes to find shards of pottery on the grass. Luella and Duncan scrambled for the silver coins on the ground. Excitedly, Penny bent over to help pick up the money.

"Good smashing!" said Luella.

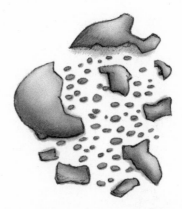

11

Breaking the Rules

When they'd scooped up every last coin, the three kids looked at each other, grinned, and began to run. They dashed through the drooping willows, down the gravel drive, and around the first bend into the winding road. They jangled noisily, with their heavy pockets banging against their legs, until suddenly it occurred to Duncan that his father would find his locked door and open window before they were back. He stopped in his tracks.

"What will he do," he asked, "when he finds me gone? My dad, I mean."

"Obviously," said Luella, "he'll come looking for you. So let's get a move on and make his conniption worth it."

They ran faster then, jangling and jingling, occasionally shouting out "Oof!" or "Ouch!" as their coin-heavy pockets bruised their thighs. They went too quickly for

Penny to pay much attention to anything on the way, though she had hoped to peek into a few of the little old shops on Main Street. Luella sped along so doggedly that she bumped into a woman pushing a stroller on the narrow sidewalk.

"Sorry," Luella called out over her shoulder. "Cute kid!"

Before Penny knew it, they were all sliding into a red leather booth at the Junction Lunch. Kay the waitress plunked down sweating water glasses almost immediately.

Penny waved shyly. "Hi," she said. "Remember me?"

"Course I do," said Kay cheerfully. "Penny, right?"

Penny nodded. "And you're Kay."

"Most days I am," laughed Kay. "What'll you kids have?"

"Everything!" said Duncan excitedly, beginning to empty his pockets onto the table in clinks and clatters.

"*Everything?*" asked Kay, furrowing her brow. "Does your dad know you're here, Duncan?"

Luella spoke for Duncan. "He sure does," she said quickly. "It's an experiment. Doctor's orders. We'll have one of everything." Luella seemed to be avoiding looking Kay in the eyes.

Penny focused on sorting her own change. She stacked the quarters carefully.

Kay squinted at the three kids. "Doctor's orders, huh?" She paused and they held their collective breath, waiting. *"Really?* You wouldn't be fibbing, now, would you?"

Luella looked up and batted her eyelashes. "Who, *me?"*

Kay chuckled. She patted each of the three kids on the head. Then she walked back to the kitchen.

"Whew!" whispered Luella once Kay was out of earshot. "I wasn't so sure she'd go for it, but either she's a sucker, or she's on *our* side."

Penny thought about this as Duncan got out a copy of the list, which his parents made him keep folded in his pocket as a reminder. *Duncan's allergies,* it said.

When Kay arrived with the first set of plates, Penny lifted up her camera to film the opening shots. She zoomed in on Kay's cheery face, then on each plate.

Duncan took a deep breath and handed the list to Luella. "You keep track, okay?" he asked a little nervously. "Here goes nothing!" Then, as Penny sat back and positioned the camera on Duncan's eager face, he reached for a spoonful of chili topped with shredded cheese and chopped onions. *"Yum!"* Penny made sure to zoom in for a close-up when he swallowed.

Duncan ate fried clams and French fries, hot fudge

and green beans, scrambled eggs and mandarin oranges that flung their juice at the glass lens of Penny's camera. He ate baked ziti and butterscotch pudding, and he washed it all down with grape soda. He even tried the house specialty—a grilled peanut butter and honey sandwich that would have given his dad a fit. He didn't attempt to eat *everything* Kay set before him, but he did sample at least one bite of every forbidden food. With a fork in one hand and a spoon in the other, he darted and danced from dish to dish, and Penny, camera in hand, did her best to keep up.

Luella was in charge of the list. With a pen Kay had lent her, she marked off ingredient after ingredient with a shout. "Wheat—check! Corn—check! Sugar—check! Beef—check! High fructose corn syrup—check! Cream and butter and jam—check, check, and check!"

Kay came by to oversee the goings-on now and then with a secret smile on her face. Periodically she recited a recipe, in case Luella missed an ingredient from the list. "There's shredded carrots in the stew. Did you get that? And pineapple in the yams." Then she'd go back to the kitchen.

Finally Luella cried out, "DONE!" and Penny set down the heavy camera with a relieved groan. According to the little red numbers on the digital display, she'd been recording for just under thirty-seven minutes—thirty-seven minutes of solid eating!

Duncan looked up, startled from his frenzied gluttony. He stared at the piece of paper in his friend's hand. He seemed puzzled.

"You're done!" she shouted again. "You have officially tasted every single food on your list. How do you feel?"

"Yeah, how do you feel?" Penny repeated, leaning in to peer at her new friend.

Duncan smiled. "I feel—" Then his eyes crossed as his stomach gave a terrible rumble, and his smile disappeared. "Actually, I feel—not so good." He rubbed his belly. "I feel awful."

As Luella and Penny watched, concerned, Duncan groaned and slumped down sideways so that he was lying flat in the booth. He let out a terrible moan and rolled onto the floor beneath the table. "I think I'm sick. I mean it. Oh, man. I'm going to *die*. And then my parents are going to kill me." He closed his eyes.

"Oh no," said Luella, sliding from the booth and kneeling beside her friend's head. She felt his forehead. It felt clammy. "Oh *no!*"

Duncan groaned again, louder, and his eyelids flickered.

Luella slapped his face and he cried out.

Penny watched in horror, frozen. This was all her fault. It had been *her* idea. "Luella!" she said. "What can we do?"

Luella said nothing. She just stared down at Duncan, horizontal on the floor beside her.

Suddenly Penny stood up in the booth. They needed a grown-up immediately. "Kay!" she shouted. "Kay, help! HELP!"

The woman ran in from the kitchen, wiping her hands with a dish towel. "What? What? Is someone choking? What *is* it?"

"Quick! Where's the nearest hospital?" cried Penny.

"Wha? Hospital? What for?" asked Kay, looking seriously worried. "What's going on?" She looked down at Duncan.

"No time to explain," cried Luella. "The hospital is all the way in North Junction. Too far. We just need to get him to Dr. Sanchez!" She pulled on his arm. "Here, help me get him up!"

"Hospital? Doctor? What are you kids saying?" asked Kay frantically. "Slow down. What happened? Did he slip and fall?"

"No!" said Penny. "He just lay down and began to moan. We think it's his allergies! There's no time to lose. We need a doctor *now*!"

Kay calmly crouched down and pulled Duncan to a sitting position. She put a hand to his forehead. "You going to be okay, Dunc? Tell me—where's it hurt?" She gently helped him back up and into the booth.

"My stomach," said Duncan, opening his eyes. "Oh, my stomach feels terrible." Then he burped and began to whimper. "I must be allergic to something after all! How will we ever know what it was?" He moaned. "It could have been *anything*."

But when Duncan burped, Kay made a strange noise, a kind of muffled bark. Looking over, Penny was shocked to realize that Kay was trying not to laugh.

Luella seemed to be thinking the same thing. "What's so funny?" she yelled at Kay. "Duncan could be *dying*!"

The waitress straightened up and wiped her hands on her apron. She looked down at Duncan sitting limply in the booth. "You do *not* have an allergy," she said, letting out a warm, rolling chuckle. "We do *not* have to bother Dr. Sanchez with this—though I'm sure Duncan's parents would prefer if we did." She waggled a finger at Penny and Luella. "For shame! You girls just took about ten years off my life, you scared me so bad."

Duncan had managed to stay in an upright position. "Honest, Kay? You think I'll survive?" he asked.

"You're fine. I'd bet the Junction Lunch on it," said

Kay. "I raised four kids of my own, you know. A mother knows." She considered this last point. "Well, *most* do, anyway."

"Then why does he feel so sick?" asked Penny, her eyes wide and her voice shaky. Her frantic fear was melting away, leaving behind a kind of tired, fluttery feeling in her chest.

"Because, silly girl, he just ate the entire lunch menu, including our five-alarm chili and some questionable beets from Tuesday's lunch special," said the waitress. "I probably shouldn't have served those."

"But look at him. He's *really* sick!" said Penny.

Duncan did look very pale.

"Of course he is," said Kay. "But he doesn't have an allergy, just a raging case of indigestion."

"Are you sure?" asked Duncan, letting out another terrible burp. "It really hurts."

"Of *course* it does," said Kay. "You've spent your life eating boiled chicken. Your poor guts don't have the first idea what to do with all those wild flavors, so they're chock-full of plights and gripes. But a body is a tough thing. It takes a fair amount of harm to kill off a healthy boy."

Duncan considered this. "Are you sure?" he asked.

"Well, I suppose you *might* be allergic—if your throat

is closing up or you're covered in hives. Can you breathe?"

"I can breathe." Duncan nodded, swallowing huge gulps of air.

"Yeah," laughed Kay. "Kinda looks that way to me. Any hives? You feeling itchy?"

"I don't think so," said Duncan. He inspected his arms and legs. "Not yet."

"I think you'll live," said Kay. "And while I should feel bad for allowing this craziness, I have to admit I'm pleased as punch to see you eating like a normal kid. I'd say you're as fine as anyone could be after a meal like that."

"Fine?" asked Penny.

"Fine!" repeated Luella. "You hear that, Dunc? You're fine!"

Duncan smiled weakly, though his joy was tempered by his frequent burps, so Kay mixed him up a cloudy glass of warm water and baking soda. Duncan made a face as he drank it. He complained that the mixture tasted worse than Benadryl, but it seemed to help a good deal.

Penny was concerned that perhaps they didn't have enough money to leave a very big tip after causing Kay so much trouble, but the waitress just chuckled at them.

"Oh, don't you worry about the pennies, darlin'. Getting to see a hungry boy full for the first time in his life is its own reward."

As the three friends left the Junction Lunch, Penny noticed Dijon parked in front of a very official-looking building called the Department of Sanitation/City Planner/School Board. She looked around, but neither of her parents was anywhere to be seen. So she trundled along home with Luella and Duncan. They only stopped once so Duncan could briefly lie down again along the side of the road.

Duncan looked up at the two girls from his bed in the weeds and said, "Thanks, guys. I'd never have been brave enough to do this without you."

It made Penny feel very, very good, though it seemed a funny thing to be happy about—not at all like something that would happen in a book. Unless maybe the book was *Mrs. Piggle-Wiggle*.

Back at the Whippoorwillows, they had another stroke of amazing luck. Duncan's dad was still sound asleep in a dark room, recovering from his anxious headache (or maybe getting ready for the next one).

The next morning Penny and Luella knocked three times on Duncan's door, but nobody came to answer it.

"Let's just hope Mr. Weatherall's head didn't explode

when he saw that video," said Luella, shaking her head with worry.

Just as Penny and Luella turned to walk away, the door swung open and Duncan stuck his head out. "I can't play," he whispered, "not right now. But I wanted to tell you both—things are okay. I think. I showed Dad the video, and he freaked out at first and called Mom, so then she came home from work in a rush and watched it too. After that they took me to see the doctor, just in case, but it turned out okay. Dr. Sanchez is on our side. She watched the video, laughed at my parents, and gave me a lollipop when we left. Mom and Dad were so relieved, they let me eat it!"

"Oh, good!" cried Penny.

"All *right!*" said Luella.

"Yeah." Duncan grinned. "And we're going to try ordering pizza for dinner tonight. My very first pizza ever!" He looked elated but kept his voice low. "It *is* good. Everything's very good. But right now I have to run. My poor old dad. He's feeling kind of fragile."

12

LIKE REGULAR LIFE

After that Luella and Penny tried to think of something fun to do.

"Maybe we should go see if anyone else wants to play," said Luella. "There are other kids who live here too, you know." She thought for a minute. "But Alice is away at camp, so it's mostly my dopey sister and her friends who come over, plus some little preschool munchkins who hang around."

"I wouldn't mind meeting your dopey sister," said Penny, who didn't know the first thing about sisters.

Luella shook her head and frowned. "Better to keep our distance. Teenagers are awful. Bea just sits in her room talking on the phone and reading books about kissing with dumb pictures of lipstick girls looking sneaky on their covers. Sometimes the girls have their heads cut off." Luella made a disgusted face. "Plus, whenever I *do*

run into Bea, she asks me to go and get her something—
a snack or her flip-flops or something. I'm *never* going to
be a teenager."

Penny wasn't sure how Luella planned to manage
that, but before she could ask, Luella said, "Let's just play
by ourselves today."

That sounded fine to Penny. "Okay," she said. "Didn't
you say something about dressing up a dog?"

Unfortunately, they didn't have a dog handy, so
instead they decided to sit on the porch and read books
about everything but kissing.

Penny, who'd run up to fetch the copy of *Return to
Gone-Away* she had just started reading, was surprised
when Luella came out of her apartment with a huge stack
of library books about people who were explorers or
scientists or magicians.

"I've never read a book like this before," said Penny,
leafing through a book about a woman named Amelia
who flew planes. "Except really boring ones my tutor
made me read for lessons." She stopped to stare at the
pictures. "I usually read books about people who seem
magical or different from me."

Luella, who had been taking a quick peek at Penny's
book, held it up in the air. "You mean like *this* one, about a
girl who moves one summer from the city to the country

and ends up in a weird old house hanging out with some oddball characters?" There was a tiny smile at the corner of her mouth as she waved the book at Penny. "Magical or different?"

"Oh," said Penny. "Hmm. I hadn't thought about it quite like that."

"Yeah," said Luella with a laugh. "You should try reading nonfiction sometime. It's more interesting. Less like real life!"

Penny laughed back. "Okay, let's swap!"

They did just that, and for several hours the girls settled into comfortable reading spots. Luella sat on the porch swing and Penny settled down in the big wicker chair, and they didn't say much to each other. When it got hot, Luella went in for two glasses of lemonade. At lunchtime they went upstairs, where Dirk made them elaborate grilled cheese sandwiches full of mushrooms and grilled onions and spicy mustard. But when they were done eating, they came back down. Oddly, nobody else came or went much. It was as though they had the Whippoorwillows all to themselves.

Penny liked leafing through Luella's books and stopping on the old photographs. Once in a while the girls would stop reading to chat about nothing in particular, or to ask each other questions or share a joke.

Late in the afternoon Penny stopped reading to gaze up at the cloudless summer sky and listen to the porch swing creak and notice a bee buzzing. She glanced over at her friend, who seemed engrossed in a book called *The Way Things Work,* and wondered how it could be that she was not the least bit bored.

In fact, Penny was so content, and Luella was so content, that for a number of days the two girls kept mostly to themselves and stayed busy, if you could call it busy, doing nothing and everything, the way friends do. They sat in their fort beneath the waving willow fronds, and they swung on the porch swing. They lounged around in a falling-apart hammock behind the house and listened as Old Joe practiced playing the fiddle one morning. They played Uno under a tree and drew pictures of what they thought they might look like when they grew up and

were famous actresses and/or fairies and/or vampires and/or rock stars.

Duncan joined them for the Uno, but he absolutely refused to draw pictures of himself as a fairy or an actress, and grumbled off, saying, "We *have* to get some more boys around here."

Four days, seventeen scratches, two bruises, and three mosquito bites later, the two girls were upstairs helping Dirk shuck corn for a salad when Penny suddenly remembered something. "Hey—back before Duncan stopped being fragile, weren't we supposed to go get penny candy?"

"Oh yeah!" said Luella. "I totally forgot. Yikes! You still haven't been to the General Store! We should fix that right away, but we'll need money." Since Penny's life savings was now gone and Luella was still saving for a skateboard, the two friends ran directly down to *borrow* some money from Luella's mother's change jar. Penny didn't think it was a good time to ask *her* parents for any money.

By now Penny had been inside Luella's apartment a few times, briefly, and each time she'd wondered at the odd emptiness of it: the white walls with nothing on them, the stark few bits of furniture, the absent parents. It did not feel to Penny like a place where people lived, and she had been more than happy to roam outside or to invite Luella to play upstairs.

From time to time, darting in and out downstairs, they *had* run into Bea on her way to the bathroom or getting a snack in the kitchen. One time she yelled bossily from her room, "Hey, Luella! Grab me a soda, will you?" But mostly it seemed like she wasn't there at all.

Today, when Penny and Luella stepped inside, the place looked different. A huge easel with a giant canvas on it stood in one corner of the front room. On the floor was a tarp covered in splatters of every color imaginable. On the tarp were brushes and tubes of paint. The room smelled funny, in a chemical way.

In front of the easel was a surprise—a person, a woman.

"Hi, Lu!" said the woman, who had her back to the girls. She held a brush in one hand and a palette in the other. She dabbed and daubed at the canvas in front of her. She didn't turn around. "Painting furiously. Can't stop. Talk later," she said.

"Okay, Mom," said Luella. "But you *said* you wanted to meet Penny someday, and you're home today, and *this* is Penny, and today *is* someday. Penny, this is my mom." She added in a whisper to Penny, "I'll be right back. With *moola.*"

Then she left Penny to stare in wonder at the scene before her.

Although Penny had visited museums on field trips with Joanna, she had never before met an artist, or seen an actual studio, which is what the living room was transformed into today.

Luella's mom turned around. She wore a pair of old denim overalls, with no shoes, and her wild black curls stood out from her head in a glorious pouf. Her skin was much darker than Luella's, and a smear of silver paint on her nose stood out brightly, almost glinting in the sunlight. As Luella's mom stepped aside, Penny saw that she was working on a picture of a horse that didn't really look like a horse. Penny wasn't sure how she knew it was a horse, but she was certain it was.

"Sorry to be rude, Penny. Didn't know we had a guest!" laughed Luella's mom.

"It's okay, Mrs. Gulson," said Penny a little shyly. "It's nice to meet you."

"Nice to meet *you!*" said Luella's mom. "But I'm not a Mrs. anybody. I'm just Abbie. Lu has been saying *such* nice things about you."

"Thanks," said Penny happily, though still quietly, "Abbie."

"Now that we're friends," said Abbie, "do you mind if I keep working?" She waved her paintbrush in the air. "The light is just right, and it won't last long. It never does."

Penny shook her head, and Abbie turned away to dab and daub, smear and splatter. Penny watched, fascinated, until Luella burst back into the room, pockets bulging.

"Ready, Penny?" she asked.

Penny didn't even have time to reply. Without turning

around, Abbie called out, "Yes, she's ready. Now go. Go. Get!" in a tone both forceful and friendly.

The girls got.

This time they didn't run. Slowly, Penny and Luella walked to town, stopping every twenty feet or so, so that Penny could notice a cardinal or remark on how pretty the blue flowers were that grew by the road. Each time Luella responded with something like "Oh, it's just a bird" or "What, *that* old weed?" But it was all new to Penny.

On Main Street, Penny stopped to peek in the windows of all the funny old storefronts they passed, which she hadn't had time for when they'd run to town with Duncan. Though there weren't very many shops, each store was well worth peering into because each was different from the next, and they were all a little strange besides.

Looking in one dusty window, Penny realized she was staring at gigantic vats of dried corn and what looked like different kinds of pellets and seeds. A woman in a cowboy hat sat behind a cash register reading a magazine, but the store was otherwise empty. Penny shifted her gaze toward the ceiling of the room and discovered an iridescent glow caused by a number of stunning wedding dresses, worn by mannequins of every size. The mannequins dangled from the ceiling so that they seemed to rise from the vats, hanging over them like ghosts in the dim, their silken arms covered with corsages. Penny stepped back so she could read the sign over the shop's door, and she laughed out loud to discover that it said FUGATE'S FEED SHOP AND BRIDAL STORE.

"What's so funny?" asked Luella. When she saw what Penny was giggling at, she said, "Oh, *that*. Yeah. The Fugate family ran the feed shop, a regular old feed store, but then Mr. Fugate married Noelle. Noelle was a regular seamstress, but she'd always dreamed of making wedding dresses. So since they already had the store, she just moved her nicest dresses on in. Now everyone in town goes there for their dresses *and* their oats. Noelle does other kinds of sewing too. Last year she made me a Halloween costume. I was Furious. Mom traded her a painting for it."

"Neat," said Penny, though she couldn't really imagine what a Furious costume might look like. Lots of red, she guessed.

After that the girls passed a store called the Praise God the Lord Hot Dog Shack. The front of the building was decorated with extremely happy sausages wearing halos, and the tables in the front window were full of people munching away.

Luella whispered, "Ramona Smith is superstrict. You can't talk on a cell phone in there, or interrupt, or fight, or cuss, or anything like that. If you do, she'll kick you out! One time my mom got thrown out for not saying grace before she ate. But wow, does Ramona make a good slaw dog. The recipe came to her in a vision!"

Penny stared through the window. The inside walls of the shack were covered in colorful scribbles. What the words said Penny could not quite make out, but she did see a very skinny woman with her hair in a tight little bun stirring a boiling kettle and beaming into the steam. The woman looked up and waved. Penny waved back.

Behind the hot dog shack was a playground made of old traffic lights and street signs, wrapped and planted around lots of huge tires. Some kids were climbing and jumping around on the lampposts, and Penny thought it looked like lots of fun. But Luella kept walking and said, "Baby stuff," with a wave of her hand. So Penny ran to catch up and made a mental note to come back later.

Next to the playground was the reason for their trip—the General Store.

"Look! We're here!" cried Luella, tossing a hand in the air and climbing the three steps to the door.

Penny followed, noticing that each stair was painted a different color. Red, white, blue.

Luella pushed open the door, and a bell rang out in a nice chingy way. "Hey, Mr. Milstein!" she called out.

Penny found herself in a wonderful room, surrounded by a wild array of *stuff*. There were bins of nails beside bolts of fabric, bottles of perfume and very old greeting cards, sprinklers and red bandannas. Everything was jammed together in any old order, and it all smelled vaguely of peppermint gum and rust and old paper and years and years of dust.

Penny was mesmerized. She knelt to examine the large bins of candy under the front counter. Then she looked up to find herself staring into the gentle, lined face of Mr. Milstein.

"What'll it be, gals?" the old man asked, handing each of them a brown paper bag before they could even answer. "Penny candy, I'm guessing?"

"You got it," said Luella. "And maybe a double deluxe Moon Pie or three, if we've got enough money. We need to fortify ourselves if we're going to walk to the caves and look for Blackrabbit's gold. I'm feeling lucky today."

"*Gold? Caves?*" Penny asked Luella. This was the first she'd heard of either.

Luella shrugged. "I figured we're already halfway there, might as well."

"I suppose," said Mr. Milstein with a wink at Penny, "*somebody* has to find it, right?"

Luella scoffed. "Not *somebody*. Me!"

"All right. All right," said the old man. "*You.*"

Mr. Milstein turned his attention to Penny. "Don't believe I've had the pleasure," he said. "Who might you be?"

"That's Penny," said Luella.

Mr. Milstein smiled. "Good to meet you, Penny. Though I had a wretched neighbor named *Miss* Penny when I was little. We used to call her Miss Penny Dreadful behind her back, on account of the fact that she swore like a drunk pirate. *You* aren't a Dreadful, are you?"

Penny shook her head shyly. *She* certainly didn't swear like a drunk pirate.

"What's a penny dreadful?" asked Luella.

"Oh, naturally, you girls are too young to know," said Mr. Milstein. "Penny dreadfuls were—"

"A kind of magazine!" said Penny eagerly. "I found some that used to belong to Aunt Betty. They're full of adventure and excitement."

"Oho!" said Mr. Milstein, amused. "So you're familiar, are you? Maybe you *are* a bit like a penny dreadful, after all. You seem pretty adventurous yourself."

Penny blushed.

"You know who likes adventure, don't you?" said Mr. Milstein suddenly. "Jasper!"

"Jasper!" cried out Luella, looking quickly around the shop. "Is she here?"

"Sure is! Koko's at some kind of summer camp for musical toddlers because when she hangs around here, she gets into the nail bin, but Jasper's in the back somewhere playing jacks, I think. I bet she'd rather go to the caves. Oh, Jasper! JASPER!" he yelled, and his bellow was surprisingly loud for such a gentle old man.

"Who's Jasper?" asked Penny, counting out gumdrops. "Who's Koko?"

"They're my granddaughters," said the old man. "Jasper's about your age. You'll like her. Everyone does." He winked and then yelled again, "JASPER!"

"Oh," said Penny.

Luella smiled and nodded in agreement. "She's in my class at school. Jasper's great! The best!"

When Luella said this, Penny suddenly felt strange—grumpy in a greenish kind of way. It took her by surprise because for days and days now she'd been feeling sunny and good. There was no reason why she should feel this way. And she *did* want to make more new friends. But . . .

Penny was new to jealousy, so she couldn't put her finger on exactly what her grumpy, snaky feeling was.

She only knew she did not want to meet this Jasper girl.

"Jasper's fun!" added Luella. "She made up her very own secret code. She has a pet skunk!"

Penny pretended to be absorbed in filling her bag with licorice whips. "That's weird," she said quietly.

Luella scowled at her cheerfully, in a way only Luella could manage. "Only because *you* haven't met the skunk!"

When Jasper emerged from the storeroom, Penny was instantly certain she didn't want to make friends. Jasper, in her faded sundress, red sneakers, and long auburn braid, was none other than the Possum Girl, and while Penny was growing to appreciate things like tangled hair and bare feet and trouble, she was pretty certain that she would never think it was fun to play with a squashed possum.

Penny sat and rooted through some brightly colored jawbreakers as Jasper and Luella high-fived each other. She fingered chocolate coins as they chattered about which teacher each of them was hoping to have when school began in the fall.

Penny had nothing to contribute since she had no idea what any of the teachers' names were. As she listened to their chatter, a thought struck her—what if she wasn't in Luella's class? Or what if she didn't like her teacher, or her new school?

Suddenly Penny—who had been perfectly happy a few moments before—had a great number of things to worry about, and all of them had arrived with Jasper.

After a few minutes Luella finally bothered to introduce Penny and Jasper to each other. Penny said a quick "Hey" and then looked back down at her candy as if there were something terribly interesting hiding among the gumdrops. Neither Luella nor Jasper noticed her lack of interest, which only made Penny feel worse.

Of course Jasper wanted to join them for a walk. *Of course* she'd come along to the caves. Penny felt tight in her chest. She held up her candy bag and nudged Luella, who had the money. "How much?" she asked Mr. Milstein.

"Oh, no charge today!" said Mr. Milstein, waving the girls out the door. "Have a nice day, ladies!"

"Hey, thanks! That's great!" said Luella. "Isn't that great, Penny?"

"Great," muttered Penny. She shoved a caramel into her mouth.

There was nothing for Penny to do but follow the other girls from the store. She chewed in frustration and listened to Luella and Jasper giggle. The sidewalk wasn't wide enough for three, and it was Penny who fell behind.

BOOK FOUR

PLIGHTS AND GRIPES

13

More Country Cooking

Walking behind Luella and Jasper gave Penny plenty of time to think cranky thoughts. She wondered if Luella knew that her friend played with dead animals. She guessed not, and wondered if Luella would still be friends with Jasper once she found out. After that she wondered what Jasper had *done* with the possum when she got to wherever she'd been going. Penny couldn't imagine. She noticed that Jasper's braid, bouncing along ahead of her, was lopsided and fastened with a dirty rubber band. One of her red high-tops was untied.

Penny no longer found the birds and flowers so lovely. She noticed that the store windows were dingy. The people they passed on the street all looked angry. One man was grumbling out loud as he tried to start his car. The paint on the buildings looked peelier than before.

The farther they walked, the more grouchy Penny

became. She wasn't sure if she was more mad at Jasper for horning in on her day with Luella, or more disgusted by the general idea of a dead possum. The two feelings had gotten all tangled together so that she didn't know what she was feeling anymore. In any case, it was not good, and she did not want to hunt for gold with Jasper, or do anything else with her either. Penny kicked a rock.

Sooner, rather than later, Penny *might* have been won back by the sunny day and the pleasure of eating a bag-ful of candy. Her jealousy and her disgust *might* have faded quickly into the landscape around her. Despite herself, Penny was intrigued when Jasper began to talk about her pet horse, Mr. Clop, and about how the three of them could all go riding one day. But then the three girls happened upon a squashed mouse lying in the road.

Jasper stopped to kneel and examine the dead thing up close. Penny peered over the other girl's shoulder, and her stomach turned when she saw there were tiny mag-gots wriggling in the animal's eyeholes. She looked away. How could Jasper stand it? It was revolting.

"Oh!" exclaimed Jasper, crouching closely to inspect the dead rodent. "What a waste!" Then she took off one sneaker and wrapped the tiny mouse gently in a dirty sock.

Penny stared. Luella wrinkled her nose.

"Sorry, guys," said Jasper, putting her shoe back on.

"Maybe I can go treasure hunting with you another time, but right now I should probably get this little guy home before he really starts to smell." To Penny she said, "My house is that way," and pointed down a narrow, pebbly dirt side road choked with trees. "But it was nice to meet you!" she said with a friendly wave.

"Oh—okay," said Penny, surprised by Jasper's sudden departure. "It was—umm—nice to meet you too. And yeah, uh, maybe another time."

"That'd be great!" said Jasper, with a smile so kind and warm that Penny felt a little bit bad at how relieved she was to see her wave goodbye.

Her relief was short-lived because almost immediately Luella was running after Jasper, calling, "Hey! Wait! Wait up, you goof! We'll walk you home! A walk is a walk, and we can look for Blackrabbit's gold any old day. Come on, Penny!"

Penny watched Luella run off after Jasper. She didn't know what to do. The last thing she wanted was to follow this strange girl and her dead mouse, but she couldn't bear to walk away from Luella either, and she wasn't sure she could find her way back alone anyway. She followed Luella slowly toward Jasper, frowning all the way.

When she caught up with the other two girls, Jasper's

face lit up. "You guys are so nice," she said. "If you want me to, I'll make us all lunch. My mom and dad started a pot of meaty surprise in the Crock-Pot before they left for work this morning. I bet it's nice and tender by now."

"Um, I don't know," said Penny, not liking the sound of lunch with Jasper any more than the sound of *meaty surprise*. "I don't think I'm supposed to eat at a stranger's house." This was true, in theory, though lately she'd been doing all kinds of things she wasn't sure she was supposed to do.

Luella argued, "Jasper's not a *stranger*, Penny!"

Penny could think of no further excuse, so she ended up following Luella and Jasper down yet another winding road and out of town. As she trudged along glumly behind Jasper and Luella, past dilapidated houses and rusted old cars, Penny looked nervously at the sock Jasper carried so carefully and knew that no matter what, she would not be able to choke down a bowl of meaty surprise. Penny forgot her jealousy as she thought about the mystery lunch awaiting her.

It didn't help that when she sped up to rejoin Luella and Jasper, she heard Jasper say, "Yeah, I actually froze a few of the ones I found last winter. I just knew I wouldn't be able to put them up until spring."

Penny cringed.

It also didn't help that when they walked up the steps of Jasper's house, the house was all dark and spooky-looking. It sat alone on the edge of a large green field, far from neighbors. Large elm trees cast shadows over the house, so that when the three girls arrived at the top of the porch steps, what sunlight there was fled their shoulders. Jasper reached for the door, and a cacophony of noises assaulted Penny's ears: hoots and shrieks and barks and whines and yowls!

Penny held back as Jasper entered the house and Luella followed. The screen door slammed shut behind them. They appeared to have forgotten all about her.

Alone on the porch, Penny tried to remind herself that Luella was her friend. There was no reason to feel bad. Luella was her friend. Luella was her friend. Penny knew that. She did. Luella *was* her friend.

Staring at the closed screen door and listening to the animal noises, Penny wished she could turn around and go home, but if she didn't go inside soon, Luella would probably tease her forever. Penny took a deep breath and placed a hand on the door handle. She opened it with a creak and stepped gingerly inside, where she found a disconcerting menagerie. An owl flapped about her head as a squirrel scampered past her feet. A cat curled and slunk upon the mantelpiece, and two tired-looking dogs loped in from another room, tongues lolling. A skunk shuffled off into the dining room.

Penny could hear other noises too, and she wondered if these animals would also become "meaty surprises." Surely even a family who ate possum wouldn't cook *dogs*, would they?

Penny fought through the sea of creatures, found her way to the kitchen, and wrestled open a plastic gate to join the others. Jasper, wearing a pair of yellow rubber gloves, appeared to be washing the maggots from the dead mouse in a big kitchen sink. "Sorry about the gate!" she called out. "It's to keep my sister, Koko, from poking the babies."

"Babies?" asked Penny, puzzled. Then the smell hit her. All through the room a strong scent was wafting, a deep tomatoey odor filled with spices Penny couldn't identify. It was a rich, warm smell—a delicious smell.

Penny took a deep whiff. "Is *that* meaty surprise?"

Jasper looked over from her unpleasant job and said, "Yup, doesn't it smell great? My grandmother's recipe from Hungary. She taught my mom to cook it." Jasper went back to scrubbing. "You'll never guess what the surprise is," she laughed.

Penny inhaled again. She was almost certain she knew what the surprise was, so she was confused. She found it hard to believe that stewed possum smelled so scrumptious.

"Hey, Penny, look at this," called Luella from the floor, distracting Penny from her thoughts. "You have to see this!"

Penny knelt down beside her friend. When she peeked inside the box, her grouchiness faded away and she let out a soft coo. "Oh," she said. "Ohhhhhh!"

"I know, right?" Luella agreed, reaching down to stroke the baby animals cuddled into an old sweater at the bottom of the box. They were nestled together sweetly, and though they made small hissing noises at the sight of Luella's big hand, Penny couldn't resist reaching for them too.

"What are they?" she asked, looking at the squirmy pink-and-gray animals.

"Possums," said Luella. "Baby ones."

Staring at the babies, Penny sat back on her heels, puzzled. What did this mean? As much as she didn't really like Jasper, Penny simply could not believe that she intended to eat these adorable creatures too. She knew, in theory, that every hamburger or chicken nugget started out its life as a baby of one kind or another, but she couldn't see how anyone could raise an animal like this and then throw it into a Crock-Pot.

She looked over at Jasper, who was wrapping the cleaned mouse in paper. Penny could no longer keep her thoughts to herself. "You aren't—you aren't really going to *eat* them, are you?" she asked.

Jasper stopped wrapping and stared at Penny like she was crazy. "Huh?" she said. "What are you *talking* about?"

"I mean, they're just babies . . . ," Penny continued.

Luella snorted a laugh. "Well, young flesh *is* tender."

Penny turned to her, horrified.

Luella burst out laughing. "*Joking,* I'm joking!" she said. "What *are* you talking about? Why would anyone eat a baby possum?"

Penny stammered, and looked from Luella to Jasper. "B-b-but the meaty surprise—"

Jasper looked truly flabbergasted. "Of *course* I'm not going to eat them! I'm going to *keep* them! In case you can't tell, we like animals around here. A lot. We're vegetarians. My mom's a vet, for gosh sakes. My dad's a wildlife photographer. Koko was named after a gorilla."

Luella stared at Penny. "Jeez, Penny, *really?* You *really* thought that?"

"I just thought—well, I saw you carrying a dead possum," Penny blurted out. "Last week, when we were first driving into town. And I thought—"

"You thought wrong," said Jasper. "I was rescuing a family of baby possums. *These* baby possums. Someone hit and killed the mother, and I noticed that her belly was rippling when I walked past, so I took her home to save the little bitty ones inside her pouch. It was the easiest way to carry them all. And there they are," she added, pointing to the box. "Possums are marsupials, you know."

Penny blushed as she continued. "Then what about the mouse?" she asked, gesturing to the neatly wrapped mouse in Jasper's hand. "*That's* not a pet. Is it? What are you going to do with *that?*"

"Ugh! *Gross!*" said Luella with a shiver. "She's not going to *eat* it."

But Jasper seemed to think it was a fair question. "Now *that*," she admitted thoughtfully, "that *is* a little weird. Even my mom thinks so. But I don't care. I just decided it's nicer to bury roadkill than to let them rot and get chewed up by other animals or run over by a trillion cars until they turn into hairy dried pancakes on the pavement." As she said this, she fitted the wrapped mouse into a cardboard box she had waiting on the counter beside the sink. "I have a little graveyard out back. My mom calls it my death collection."

Luella snorted. "That *is* a little bananas, Jasper. I'm

not going to lie." She turned to Penny and added, "You'll get used to Jasper's obsession. I remember one time, in first grade, Jasper brought in a huge collection of dead bugs, all pinned to a corkboard, for show-and-tell. Mrs. Johnson just about hit the roof! It was great."

Penny couldn't help giggling.

"Yeah, it was pretty crazy," said Luella. "But *you*, Penny, are even crazier! Did you really think she'd eat a dead, maggoty mouse? Who would *do* that?"

Penny blushed. "So then, all those *other* animals . . ." She motioned to all the beasts panting and scraping and chattering on the other side of the plastic baby gate.

Jasper burst into peals of laughter, a musical sound. "Those are my pets, of course—at least for a while!" She waved toward the dogs and the squirrels and the snuffly skunk. "That's Rudolpho and Jim and Old Blue and the scamper twins, Chitter and Chatter. And *that*," she added, pointing up at the owl, "is Who. I rescued all of them. They were all hurt when I found them. My mom helps me with medicine and stuff, but I feed them and bathe them and take care of them myself until they're ready to go back into the woods."

"Wow," said Penny. "I've never known anyone with a pet owl before. I've never even read a *book* about anyone with a pet owl."

"I bet you never knew anyone with a pet horse either," said Luella.

"Well, no," admitted Penny, "but *that* I've read a lot of books about."

"Oh," said Jasper. "Wait until you meet Mr. Clop! He's why we have to live all the way out here on the edge of town, so he has space to run."

"And the things you froze last winter?" asked Penny, giving up completely but still curious about the misunderstanding.

"Oh, you mean the birds I was talking about earlier? They flew into a closed window last December, but the ground was too hard to bury them deep enough that the dogs wouldn't dig them up again," said Jasper. "So I saved them for spring in our deep freeze. My folks nearly killed me. My dad unwrapped one by accident, thinking it was a burrito. Boy, was *he* surprised!"

"Ha!" added Luella.

Penny looked down at the baby possums. They'd stopped hissing and squirming for a minute, and one even let her lay a hand on his back. She could feel his heart beating through his whole body. "I feel stupid," she said. "I'm sorry. I just figured with all those dead animals around, the meaty surprise was—"

Jasper laughed even louder. "The surprise in meaty

surprise is that there's *no meat*," she explained. "It's beans and veggies and tomatoes and stuff."

"To be honest," added Luella thoughtfully, "people around here *do* make varmint stew sometimes. Full of possum and squirrel and other stuff too. I've tried it, and it's okay—"

Now it was Jasper's turn to be grossed out. "Ew, Luella. Now *that's* gross!" she said, reaching into a cabinet for three bowls. "Right, Penny?"

Penny nodded at her new friend. "*Disgusting,*" she said with a happy smile. "Let's eat!"

14

WHAT WORK IS

The next day Penny's father intercepted her on her way to the front door after breakfast and informed her that she was not allowed to leave the house until she had finished unpacking the last of her boxes and gotten her room in order. "I mean it," he said. "You need to do your fair share around here, Penny. Starting today."

"Can't I do it later?" begged Penny. "Luella is waiting! *Pleeeease?*"

"Well then, she can wait a little longer," said Dirk. "You're becoming a slob, and I won't have it. I'm putting my foot down about this."

Penny stopped arguing. "Really?" she asked, intrigued. Her father had never noticed the state of her room before in her life. He'd also never put his foot down. "Why?"

"Because this place is getting to be an absolute *disaster*," he insisted. "I mean, you haven't even unpacked all your clothes yet, and your stuff is beginning to creep out into the hallway and the living room. We don't have Josie to clean up after us anymore, and everyone has to work a little harder. Look over there!"

He pointed to a brown stuffed bear that was, indeed, peeking out into the hallway, and then to a pink sweat-shirt on the floor at his feet. Dirk tapped his foot beside the shirt impatiently until Penny leaned over and picked it up, revealing Dirk's own discarded newspaper on the floor beneath it. She looked up at her father.

"Yes, well, ahem," said Dirk, bending over to retrieve his paper. "As I was saying, we *all* have to pitch in." He folded the paper and stuck it under his arm.

"Jeez," said Penny, trying out her best Luella voice. "I've been very busy."

"Well, good for you. I'm glad you're finding things to do," said her father. "But I'm here all day in this mess, alone, and *I* get sick of looking at it."

"Where *is* Mother, anyway?" asked Penny.

"She ran out of the house at the crack of dawn today. Said something about not wanting to be late for her first day. I asked her where exactly she was going, but she refused to tell me. She said it was a surprise," said Dirk, heading back to the kitchen to tie on an apron. "Al-though, I have a sneaking suspicion."

Penny had suspicions of her own, though she almost couldn't believe them. Since she didn't seem to have a choice in the matter, Penny returned to her room, where she found she actually sort of enjoyed organizing her bookshelves, hanging pictures on her walls, folding her clothes neatly, and arranging her art supplies.

As she worked, she listened through the open doors of the apartment to her father clattering in the kitchen. Things sizzled and popped on the stove, and periodically Dirk yelled through the apartment, calling out interesting snippets he was reading in the *Junction Sun* while he waited for things to boil and brown and bake.

"Hey, Penny! Old Man Gettinger found four teenagers goofing around the water tower with spray paint last week," he said. "Made them all paint the tower for punishment, then took the kids home and had them do his barn too. Ha! Good for him!"

"That's nice, Dad," Penny would call out in response. She didn't listen carefully to anything he said since he didn't seem to be saying much.

When at last she was done, she stepped back to survey her kingdom. She was pleased at how nice her box collection looked lined up on the windowsill beneath the pink curtains. Her old stuffed animals looked just right sitting on the iron bed. Her old room had been bigger, but somehow this room matched the way Penny felt on the inside. This was funny, given that most of the things were Aunt Betty's. A spray of ivy waved hello to her from just beyond the window.

Penny heard the door open and shut. Her mother's voice joined her father's in the kitchen, and Penny left her room and headed to the kitchen for lunch. There she found Delia, dressed in a rather un-Delia-like ensemble of Dirk's jeans and a brown work shirt, sitting at the table smelling funny.

"Hi, honey," Delia said.

"Where were you, Mother?" asked Penny, obviously examining her mother's attire.

"Oh, nowhere special. Just at work," said Delia. "A little part-time job I found." She looked mildly embarrassed, but also proud.

"What *kind* of a job?" asked Penny, pulling out a chair and sliding into it.

Delia smiled and sighed. "I don't know why I'm being so secretive about it." She stood up straight and said proudly, "You are looking at the very first garbagewoman in the history of Thrush Junction. I'm a pioneer!"

Dirk stopped stirring. He turned with his spatula aloft and his eyes wide. "Wow! You really did it!"

"I did indeed," said Delia. "What do you think?"

Dirk bowed to his wife, flourishing with his spatula. "Delia, you are a woman of many surprises."

Delia beamed, her cheeks rosy and her eyes bright.

Penny nodded, but she couldn't help asking, "Isn't it kind of—I don't know—stinky?"

"It's not so bad, actually," said Delia. "There's a smell, that's for sure, but you get used to it after the first hour or so. Plus, I'll get a decent health plan for the whole family. I quite enjoyed myself, if you want to know the truth. I met lots of nice people and learned the lay of the land. I even got a tip from one nice lady for carrying her trash around from the backyard." She sighed. "I fear I'm not terribly good at it yet. I'm slow. You'd be surprised at the skills and the strength required. But I'll get better. And stronger." Delia flexed her arm muscles and grinned.

Dirk returned to his cooking. Over his shoulder he called out, "I'm sure you'll be great!"

"Yeah," added Penny. "And now we don't have to worry about the house anymore. We can stay and not think about the money." She unfolded her napkin and set it neatly in her lap, thinking that it was nice to have the problem solved, even if it *did* mean her mother would have to smell bad on a daily basis.

Delia's brow wrinkled as it had in the offices of

Donsky & Donsky. "Well, I'm not sure this totally solves our problem. It's *a* job, but I don't think it'll be *enough* of a job. So I still need to get another, unless our old house rents out soon." She sighed again. "I do have another interview—this afternoon, for something secretarial . . . but enough of this talk. What's for lunch? I'm *starving!*"

"*Another* job?" asked Penny.

"Lunch!" cried Dirk. He whipped around from the stove and set a plate of turkey hash in front of his wife. "*Voilà!*" he said. "For the working girl." Then he kissed Delia on the top of her stinky head. "I'm very proud of you, darling." He turned around to fix plates for Penny and himself, and before he'd turned back around, Delia was shoveling in the hash.

Watching her mother eat, Penny was both impressed and startled. Her mother's perfect manners were still in place—napkin in the lap, mouth closed demurely as she chewed—but Delia ate like a movie in fast-forward. It wasn't until there was nothing left on her plate that she looked up with a fork in one hand and pleading eyes. "Mmph?" she asked.

Dirk laughed. "More?"

Delia nodded as she swallowed, and Penny giggled into her potatoes. Delia laughed herself, and said, "I guess I worked up something of an appetite."

"I'm delighted you're enjoying my hash. Pretty good, right?" Dirk proudly shoveled another portion onto his wife's plate. Then he plopped down a biscuit. "I baked biscuits too! Me, a baker!" He hovered with raised eyebrows until Delia took a bite.

"Scrumptious!" said Delia, swallowing her bite. "Are there currants in them?"

Dirk nodded excitedly. "Just a crazy idea I had!"

"Dirk, I had no idea you had such talent in the kitchen! You're certainly better at it than I ever have been."

Penny had to agree. Her mother's cooking was nowhere near as good as this. She took another bite of biscuit dripping with honey.

"Thanks," said Dirk. "I wish I could take *all* the credit, but really, your great-great-aunt Betty concocted some remarkable recipes. Mostly I'm just following her directions, and enjoying myself quite a lot."

"Maybe," said Delia with a thoughtful look on her face, "there's something you could cook and sell. A lot of people around here seem to do that, sell jams and jars and cakes and things."

"But then," said Dirk, "it wouldn't be fun anymore. It would become *work*." He scowled at the last word. "Which I'd probably mess all up, not having a mind for business. Though I probably should get a job, shouldn't I? Hardly seems fair for you to be slaving away at—well, garbage, when I'm here just enjoying myself."

Delia shook her head. "No. You're working too. You are! Cooking and gardening and running the house and watching out for Penny. Someone has to do it, and you do it all so well. It counts for a lot. Besides, there's not any good work to be had around Thrush Junction, really."

"I'm glad you think I'm holding my own," said Dirk. "But I feel bad. I'm having too much fun."

"No," answered Delia, "I *want* to do this. I wanted to move here, and it was my nutty aunt who left us this money mess to deal with, so it feels good to be doing something to help fix it." She looked from her family to the sunlit window and sat back contentedly in her chair. "And it's worth it, I think. It *is* nice here, isn't it? We are happy, aren't we?"

Penny and Dirk both nodded in quiet agreement. In the distance a single car puttered down the drive, spitting gravel. A dove cooed on the windowsill, and a wind chime changled an afternoon song. Yes, whatever the adjustments, they were all very happy here.

"I only hope we don't have to leave," said Delia, rubbing at a mark on the kitchen table with her thumb.

"We're nowhere near having the money for our first payment, and the deadline is so soon."

Penny stared at the mark her mother was rubbing into the table and thought that surely, surely things would fix themselves sooner or later. They wouldn't *really* have to leave, would they?

"I still think we should charge all those folks down in the little houses rent," said Dirk. "Who gets free rent?"

Delia shook her head emphatically. "Even if we could, I'm *not* going to go begging total strangers for money they don't have. My aunt made them a promise. But maybe the Donskys would give us a little more time." She changed the subject. "Speaking of work, how's the novel coming?"

Penny looked at her dad with a curious gaze. She hadn't seen him shuffling around with his box of papers for days.

Dirk gave a dismissive wave in the direction of his office. "Hard to say. I've got some ideas, but honestly, between the garden and the meals, and just getting to know a few of the neighbors, I haven't thought about it much. I feel busy enough without it. Speaking of which, did you know that Old Joe marched with Martin Luther King Jr.? He's quite a fellow, Joe is. Maybe I should pick his brain for stories. Civil rights. Southern history. Do some research—for my book." He stood up and began to grate lemons.

Delia smiled at her husband and stood up to set her dishes in the sink. "That's a nice idea, dear," she said. "And now, if nobody minds, I think I'll take a very hot, very long shower. I have that interview later today, and I doubt they'll be impressed if I go in smelling like this."

Penny watched her mother leave. On her way to the shower, Delia stopped off in the living room, where she put something into a carved wooden box on a high shelf. Then she disappeared into the bathroom, leaving Penny to wonder what was in the box.

Penny took note of her father, absorbed in his lemony work, and excused herself. Stealthily, she made her way to the tall built-in bookshelves in the living room. Each shelf was covered in knickknacks left by Aunt Betty. Penny cleared space on the bottom shelves for her feet. Then she climbed up and silently lifted the box down. When her father didn't pop his head out of the kitchen and the sound of her mother's shower continued, Penny took the fancy carved box to a hidden spot behind the couch, sat down on the rug, and opened it.

Inside the box was money! Piles and bunches of money! At first Penny felt relief seeing all those wadded and folded bills. What was her mother so worried about?

Then she began to count. As she did, she saw the bills were mostly small, one-dollar bills and five-dollar bills, with just a few tens and twenties folded in. The bills felt tired and thin between Penny's fingers. For some reason they made her sad. Penny counted the contents of the box and set the money aside. Then she turned her attention to the piece of paper folded neatly under the money.

The letterhead at the top of the paper said *Donsky & Donsky, Esqs.*, and beneath that were a number of notations and numbers. Penny felt sick to her stomach seeing all those numbers. It took her a few minutes to understand what she was reading. According to the piece of paper, her mother would need to pay a *very* large

number of dollars every month in order to keep the Whippoorwillows.

Penny was fairly sure that even if they scrimped and saved, it would not be enough. She wasn't sure what a part-time garbagewoman, even a very good garbage-woman, made. Penny didn't think it was very much.

Wishing she'd never opened it, Penny climbed up and set the box back on the shelf.

15

TWENT, NOT TWENT

Penny could not shake the worrisome numbers from her head. Sitting on the couch, she tried to read, but she could feel the presence of the carved box in the room. *Will we really have to move back to The City?* she wondered. *How long do we have?* At last she got up and went downstairs to knock on Luella's door. But nobody answered. *That's odd,* thought Penny. Maybe Luella had walked to town, or maybe she was at Duncan's. Penny walked quickly past the orange cottage and the pink one to Duncan's red door, thinking about how very quiet everything was today.

Nobody answered at Duncan's either, so Penny returned to her porch to idly pick flakes of paint off the top step. As she picked, she wondered for the first time if it might be possible for *her* to help her mother. Delia had said that they each had a job to do, but besides running a lemonade stand, or becoming a dancer in a pantomime like the three sisters from *Ballet Shoes*, Penny couldn't think of any way for a kid her age to make money. She sat some more, thinking and trying to suck a paint chip splinter from under her fingernail. She doubted anyone ever made any real money selling lemonade, and she thought it unlikely that there were any pantomimes in Thrush Junction.

Unable to find any sort of real distraction, Penny dangled in the porch swing and wondered how long it would be until dinnertime. She wished she could remember how to get to Jasper's house. Finally, irritated with herself for her lack of *inner resources*, Penny stomped down the steps and around to the back of the house, where she wandered out into the big garden.

She walked through patches of fragrant herbs, thinking about money. She nibbled on a handful of sweet little tomatoes the size of blueberries and considered how simple her life had been in The City. How much things had changed in such a short time! Was it really true they'd only been in Thrush Junction a little more than a week? It felt like much longer. How was it possible that in a matter of days Penny had felt more happy and more worried than ever before? She wondered—did it *always* work like this? Was good stuff always so much effort?

Lost in her thoughts, Penny failed to notice she was not alone in the garden. She didn't see that creeping behind her, at a distance of about ten feet, was a creature. A creature with velvet paws and gnashing teeth that sniffed as it followed Penny, as it padded behind her almost silently.

Penny didn't notice she was being followed until the creature suddenly pounced.

"GWAH!" growled the creature at the top of his lungs.

"Aaagch!" cried Penny in surprise.

"WAHW!" yelled the creature, baring its claws and shaking its head.

Once she was over her surprise, Penny had to stifle a laugh at the creature who roared as well as anyone can without the benefit of the letter *r*. "You're very frightening," she said, "but what are you supposed to *be*?"

"I'm a lion, king of the fowest," said a boy in a yellow costume that might have been made from a bedspread. Penny guessed he was a four-year-old lion.

To say that the lion's costume was homemade was an understatement, held together as it was with safety pins and masking tape. Around his head the boy wore a yellow moth-eaten tutu. An orange extension cord served as a tail. The boy had whiskers drawn on his face.

"WAHW!" he yelled one more time for good measure. Then, in a more subdued voice, he said, "I'm Twent." He held out a hand, and when Penny took it, he gave a very formal little shake accompanied by a dignified bow. "Today I'm Twent the lion. Who awe you?" he asked.

"I'm Penny," said Penny. "Penny the girl, I guess."

"That's a nice name," said Twent. "I've nevew met a Penny befow."

"I've never known a Trent either," said Penny.

Suddenly the very dignified little lion became enraged. "NOT TWENT!" he yelled at the top of his lungs, thumping his chest. "TWENT!" He snarled. "WAHW!"

"Um, okay, Twent," said Penny, not understanding in the least.

"That's okay," said Twent, calming down. "I shouldn't have lost my tempew. Lions can be tempewmental. I'm sowwy."

"It's okay," said Penny. "I was in a bad mood myself just a little while ago."

"Do you want to come ovew to my house?" asked Twent. "We can play Pawcheesi."

Penny looked down at the little lion for a minute and had a thought: a fun thought, a fun thought of a fun thing to do. Happily, all other concerns flew from her head.

"Wait!" she called out as she ran back through the

garden in the direction of the house. "Wait right here for just a second!"

Penny bolted up her stairs and ran through the apartment and into her room. She rifled through the closet, making a mess of the order she'd created just that morning. When she dashed back down the stairs, she wasn't Penny the girl anymore.

She trumpeted as she ran across the yard and into the garden, and when she stormed back over to Twent, the boy could hardly contain his delight.

"Not Penny the *girl*," she called as she ran toward him.

"Penny the *elephant*!" he shouted, gwowling in delight. "Oh! Let's be a pawade. Wight now! Dum-da-da-da-dum. Dum-da-deedle-dee-deedle-dee-doo!"

So they were. The two of them gwowled and trumpeted through the garden. They attempted cartwheels and sang. It was lots of fun. Penny wasn't sure why she hadn't worn her elephant costume more often.

At last the animals took a break to pant and drink some water from the pump in the herb patch.

Then Twent jumped up and said, "Come on. I have something else to show you!" Penny jumped up and followed the strange little lion home to his cottage, which turned out to be the pink one in between Duncan's red house and the shining-hair girl's orange cottage. The shining-hair girl was nowhere to be seen.

Twent threw open the door. "WAHW!" he yelled, and stalked inside. Penny followed, peering curiously around at the inside of the living room, which was decorated with all sorts of bright colors.

From a back room came the voice of a woman. "Oh, gosh, Twent. Do you *have* to be a lion today? Couldn't you maybe be something else? A monkey or a giraffe? I do so love when you're a nice quiet giraffe."

"WAHW!" cried Twent, as though his mother's suggestion were downwight ludicwous.

"Okay, okay, a lion it is," said his mother, walking into the room. When she saw Penny, her face lit up. "Why, hello! A guest! What fun!"

Penny couldn't help staring a little at the woman, who was hugely pregnant and had hair to her knees. She reminded herself that beside a makeshift lion and a talking elephant, a pregnant lady with very long hair was hardly that unusual.

"I'm Penny the elephant," said Penny with a curtsy and a giggle.

The woman curtsied right back and said, "Oh, yes, you must be the new Dewberry girl! Luella stuck her head in the door last week and mentioned she'd met you.

Goodness, you do look like your aunt. You have Betty's eyes!"

"I do?" Penny said, blinking the eyes in question. She'd never been told she had anybody else's eyes before.

The woman nodded. "I'd have stopped in to welcome you to town myself, but we were away for a few weeks. And it's so hard for me to get around with this." She patted her belly. "I figured I'd wait for the big dinner next week."

"What big dinner?" asked Penny.

The woman looked concerned. "Hasn't anyone told your folks about it yet? We have a potluck supper every summer, for everyone at the Whippoorwillows and some of our friends. You arrived just in time!"

"Oh," said Penny. "That sounds fun."

"It is, but really—nobody told you about it?"

"I don't think anyone has told us about much of anything," said Penny. "My parents haven't really gotten to know very many people at all. My mother has been hunting for a job, and my dad is writing—um—a novel and cooking a lot. He did meet Down-Betty. And Old Joe too. But he hasn't really been going out of his way to meet people yet." Penny didn't add, *because we might not be here much longer.* She couldn't bring herself to say those words. It made her feel horrible just to think them.

"Even so," said the woman, "I feel terrible. I just assumed Abbie Gulson would have given you all a proper introduction. But people do get busy. Maybe we should start all over—"

"Start over?" asked Penny.

Without further explanation, the woman left the room and then came right back in, holding her belly. She awkwardly recurtsied and said, "Why, hello there! What a pleasant surprise! How do you do? So nice to meet you! I'm Willa! And you've met Twent, of course—"

"Wait, so his name really *is* Twent? I assumed it was"— she dropped her voice to a whisper, in hopes that the little boy wouldn't lose his temper again—"actually *Trent*."

Willa laughed. "Folks always assume that when Twent introduces himself. But you see, my father's name was Trent, and he passed away some years ago. Of course I absolutely had to name my son after my dear old dad, but Jenny—that's my wife—has a little speech impediment. Can't say her r's. So since Jenny was going to end up saying Twent instead of Trent, we just named him that instead. Turns out it was a good idea, because Twent can't pronounce *his* r's any better than Jenny can." Willa laughed again.

Penny was a little confused. "Your *wife*?"

"Sure." Willa smiled happily. "Twent's other mother.

She's at work now, but you'll meet her one day soon. At the potluck, if not before!"

Penny looked over at Twent, who seemed not to be paying any attention. She had never known anyone with two mothers, but then, she'd also never known anyone with hair to her knees. Or anyone with a pet skunk. Or anyone who painted huge pictures of horses in her living room.

"That would be nice," she said. "Meeting Jenny, I mean."

"Jenny isn't around much lately," sighed Willa. "She's been working a ton of overtime to get ready for the baby. Thank goodness for the Whippoorwillows. Without the free rent here, we'd never have been able to afford another kid. But we think Twent needs a sibling. It seems lonely to be an *only*, don't you think?"

"I'm an *only*," said Penny. "I guess." She hadn't ever really thought about it like that before.

"Oh," said Willa. "I'm sorry. I didn't mean anything bad by that. It just seems a little quiet to me, growing up alone. But then, I grew up with nine brothers. So I'd like Twent to have at least one sibling."

"*Nine!*" said Penny. "Wow."

Twent looked up and frowned. "I'd *wathew* have a dog."

Willa laughed. "You'll have to settle for a sister."

Twent gwowled faintly.

"I bet it'll be nice, Twent," said Penny.

Twent bared his teeth and gwowled louder. He seemed unconvinced.

Willa laughed. "Penny, I hate to say it, but I think this little lion needs a nap. He gets like this when he's tired."

"That's fine," said Penny. "I want to go see if Luella's home now, anyway."

"Of course you do," said Willa. "Tell her hello from me. But, oh! Before you go, let me write a note to your parents explaining about the potluck." She sat down on the couch and wrote a few sentences on a little card.

"We have it out back," she explained to Penny as she wrote, "about a half mile down the path that runs beside the garden, at the picnic tables around the gazebo in the clearing. I've drawn your parents a map and written some directions, just in case, but you shouldn't have trouble finding the spot. Do come! It's a ton of fun. Very neighborly."

Penny hadn't even known there was a gazebo, but a potluck did sound fun and neighborly. "There's a gazebo?" she asked. "There's a clearing?"

"Certainly," said the woman. "Just through the woods behind the house, right near the edge of Languid Lake."

"There's a lake?"

Willa chuckled. "Well, the river has to feed into something."

"There's a *river*?" said Penny. She'd thought she and Luella had explored everything there was to explore the day they'd collected branches and vines to build their fort beneath the willows. They hadn't even scratched the surface!

"Of course there is! It cuts through the mountains. Blackrabbit River, where the miners all used to pan for gold."

Penny stared at the woman dumbly, thinking vaguely that Blackrabbit was also the name of Luella's treasure.

"You haven't seen *any* of this?" asked Willa. "All you have to do is walk back along the garden path, through the trees. What has Luella been doing with you?"

Penny shrugged. "Just playing. We built a fort one day."

Willa shook her head. "We have to show you around. The lake is wonderful. There's a dock for swimming, and a big rope swing and a zip line. Twent and I like to go there and try to catch frogs."

"What do you do with them once you've caught them?" asked Penny.

"Oh, we never catch any. Between Twent's costumes

and the fact that I'm as big as a house and as slow as a slug, the frogs are pretty safe, but it's fun to *try*. You can also *try* to catch a fish."

Willa slid the note into an envelope and said, "Give this to your parents. I'll be thrilled to meet the whole family at the picnic!"

Penny took the envelope and—stepping over the small sleeping lion in the middle of the floor—headed home.

16

IN DOWN-BETTY'S GARDEN

When Penny got home, Luella was still nowhere to be seen, so she went straight upstairs to set Willa's note on the kitchen table. Then she went to look for her father. She found him snoring on his bed, asleep beside a stack of dusty books.

"Hey, Daddy," she said, sitting down beside him. "Are you awake?"

"Huh? Guh? Wha?" Dirk asked, propping himself up on his elbows, his eyes slitted. "No."

"I have a problem," Penny said.

"Hmmm," Dirk said sleepily, lying back down. "Can it wait a little while?" His nose began to whistle.

"I don't think so," said Penny.

Dirk was sound asleep again and didn't hear her at all. Penny sat for a minute and watched her father snore, mulling. When she couldn't stand thinking any longer, she tapped Dirk on the forehead until his eyes fluttered open once more. He didn't look pleased.

"Daddy," Penny said. "I *really* like it here. I don't want to leave."

Dirk eyed his daughter grouchily. "That's funny," he said after a minute, "because I was *just* wishing you would do *just* that. Leave. For maybe, oh, I don't know—forty-five minutes?"

Penny sighed as Dirk pulled a pillow over his head. She lay down on the coverlet beside him on the other side of the stack of books, stared at a spidery crack in the ceiling, and thought to herself that Dirk was not taking things seriously enough. Perhaps growing up rich had addled his brain where money was concerned. He seemed to think that money would fall from the trees or fly in the window. Or that he would stumble into a river of money when he happened to need some.

Penny felt her eyes getting itchy, like they might be wanting to cry. She frowned at the spidery crack. *I have inner resources and I will not cry*, she thought. *Instead, I will do something.*

But what? What could she possibly do?

Penny thought back over all that had happened, about everything that had changed in their lives. She remembered The City. She remembered the day her father had come home wild-eyed. She remembered the drifts and piles of laundry. Then she remembered the well in the yard, and her wishes. She remembered the moment when the doorbell rang. She remembered signing for the telegram. Penny sat up. Too bad they had left the well behind them.

Still, she thought, *I can wish. There's nothing stopping me from wishing.*

What could it hurt? Penny crossed her fingers and squeezed her eyes shut. She held her breath and made a little wish. "I wish I could fix things," she said faintly. "I wish I knew how. I wish I had *any* idea what to do to help."

Down in the yard someone suddenly began singing a song Penny had never heard before. "*Come on and hear . . . Come on and hear . . . Alexander's ragtime band.*" It didn't sound like anyone she knew. It sounded like a record or a movie star.

Penny opened her eyes, uncrossed her fingers, stood up, and peered out the window, but she couldn't see anyone out there. The singing stopped as quickly as it had started, and Penny sat back down on the bed, disappointed.

Penny sighed. It would be nice if her father could finish his novel and sell it for lots of money so they could all stop worrying. But she didn't think that was likely since Dirk didn't seem to be writing *anything*. Idly, Penny looked down at the stack of books beside her on the bed. She ran her finger along the spines as she pondered and listened to her father snore.

Most of them were cookbooks called things like *All You Knead Is Love* and *Foods from Field and Farm*, which didn't interest Penny much. Then she noticed that the book at the bottom of the stack was called *The Money River: A Brief History of Gold Panning and Stream Mining in Eastern Tennessee*. Penny paused.

A money river? That was a funny coincidence! Or was it? Penny pulled out the book and sat up to examine it more closely.

The cover was old and dusty, with yellowed pages and funny photographs from long ago. It wasn't the kind of book Penny ordinarily read, more the sort of thing Luella liked, but she began to thumb through it. At first she was distracted by the old pictures of saloon keepers and miners in squashed hats with dirty faces, but as she flipped through the pages, she came to something more interesting.

In a chapter called "Thrush Junction's Magic Mountains," Penny read about how the hills around Thrush Junction had been the site of the very first gold rush in America. In particular, she learned that a man named Briscoe Blackrabbit had struck gold in the mountains.

He had hoarded it for himself until bandits found him and made off with his treasure. The local sheriff had caught the thieves two miles outside of town, but Blackrabbit's gold had never been recovered. The last sentence of the chapter read, "And so it was that tiny Thrush Junction kept its gold, and its secrets. . . ."

Penny cocked her head to one side and closed the book slowly. But just as she was setting it back on the stack, she noticed a tiny piece of paper sticking out. She tugged on the paper and pulled out a note! The white paper was much newer than the book, and the handwriting was fancy and old-fashioned:

A door will only open for one who turns the knob.

Penny stared at the note in her hand. Surely this was just some silly quote her aunt Betty had written down. Surely that was *all* it could be. And yet . . .

Outside in the willows the song began again. "*Come on and hear . . . Come on and hear . . .*" The voice was lilting and brassy and strong. Who *was* that?

Suddenly Penny had chills. She fingered the old note in her hands and listened to the song.

Then she tapped her father on the nose, giving him one last chance.

"Dad," she said. "*Dad!* I don't want to go back to The City. I don't want to go back to being Penelope. We need to *do* something."

"Huh?" Dirk said, rousing himself again. "Wha? You want something to *do*? I'll tell you what you can do." He spoke thickly, through a haze of sleep. "Take the big colander and pick some raspberries for me." He rolled back over into the pillow. "I meant to get them earlier, but I got tired, and . . ." He yawned again. "And now I'm a little m—" Dirk began to snore.

"That wasn't what I meant by *do*," said Penny softly, but her father didn't hear her.

So Penny quietly climbed down from the bed, clutching the note, and walked to her room. She wasn't bored anymore, or worried. Now she was thinking—hard. Carefully, she placed the note in her desk drawer. Then, in the kitchen, she found the colander in the sink. She took it and headed outside and down the stairs—thinking, thinking, thinking all the while.

When she got down to the porch, she found Luella was home at last, eating a grape Popsicle on the porch swing. Luella didn't offer to share, but she patted the swing beside her and asked, "Where have *you* been all day?"

Penny didn't sit down. "Nowhere," she said. "Right here. I just came down late because my dad made me clean my room. I looked for you. But then I went for a walk and met Twent and Willa. And *then* I was reading this old book I found."

"That's cool," said Luella. "No big deal. Twent's funny. Willa's nice. Jenny's nice too."

Penny nodded. "Where were *you?*" she asked. "I looked for you."

"Oh, my mom made me go to the dentist," said Luella. "But then she took me out for lunch to celebrate no cavities." She grinned wide, making a funny face. "I had a club sandwich and a banana split."

"Yum," said Penny, but she felt distracted.

Luella reached for the colander. "What're you supposed to do with *this?*" she asked, putting the colander on her head and raising her eyebrows at Penny.

Penny didn't laugh. She just said thoughtfully, "I'm supposed to pick raspberries."

"I'll show you where they are," said Luella. She finished her Popsicle, pocketed the stick, took off the colander hat, and stood up from the swing. "At the back end of the garden, along the path, near the apple orchard beside the woods."

"Thanks," said Penny, not really listening.

"Sure," said Luella. Then she added, "Hey, Penny?"

Penny looked up.

"Are you okay?" asked Luella. "You look a little weird or something. Serious."

Penny stared at her friend. She didn't know exactly how to answer that question. She considered telling Luella about the carved box and the unwritten novel, the empty house in The City and the diseased llamas and the Donskys and the doorknob note and the money river—and this big new crazy idea she was having. But there was too much to tell and she wasn't ready. "I'm okay," she said, looking evenly at her friend. "It's just stuff with my mom and dad."

"Oh, well, parents!" laughed Luella. "Who needs *them?*"

"Yeah," said Penny. "Who needs them. . . ." Then she said, "Hey, Luella, you know that treasure you were talking about the other day?"

Luella nodded.

"Do you think you could find it?" Penny tried hard to keep her voice light and fun, but her tongue felt tight and tense in her throat. "Really?"

Luella thought about this. "Well, I don't *know* where it is. But I've been looking a long time, so I know a lot of places it *isn't.* One of these days I'll find it, I bet. Sure. Why?"

"No—no reason," said Penny. "I was just thinking . . .

something. . . ." Then she reached for her colander. "I guess I should go get those berries now."

"Yeah," said Luella. "Last one there's a rotten egg!" She dashed down the stairs and to the garden, leaving Penny no choice but to follow.

This was actually a very good thing, because Penny had been stewing a while now, and it felt good to run. Penny chased Luella down the stairs and through the waving willows, around the house, along the path, and into the garden. Luella stopped when she came upon Down-Betty in a loose sundress and her wide-brimmed floppy hat, surrounded as usual by growing things.

Under her breath Down-Betty was singing, *"That's just the bestest band what am, honey lamb . . . Come on along . . . come on along . . ."* Her voice was surprisingly strong. It didn't sound old at all. She sang as she pulled handfuls of mint from the garden, but she looked up when she saw the girls. "Either of you girls want some mint?" she asked. "It's just about taken over the garden. Militant stuff, mint."

The girls shook their heads.

Down-Betty looked disappointed. "I didn't guess so," she said. "But no harm in asking. You kids today are spoiled, you know that? Why, when I was a girl, I'd have been delighted at a nice bunch of mint. I'd have been tickled to death at such a gift. I'd have pressed it in a book or made some fresh mint tea with it."

Luella snorted. "Why, that's not true at all, Down-Betty, and you know it! When you were our age, you weren't thinking about mint at all. You weren't wasting time making tea or pressing plants!"

Down-Betty laughed. "True, true, Luella. But an old lady is *supposed* to say things like that. Old ladies are supposed to whine about how they walked to school in the snow, uphill both ways, and about how they ate on a raw potato for a week, and gathered wood for the fire. It's just what old ladies do. If there's an instruction manual to becoming old, that's one of the very first rules, right after keeping a bowl of dusty hard candy on your coffee table."

Luella laughed at that. Penny smiled.

"So, if you weren't walking to school and collecting wood and eating raw potatoes, what *were* you doing when you were a kid?" asked Penny.

"Ha!" said Luella. "Down-Betty was busy with her trapeze and her high wire. She was covered in sequins. She was dancing and hooting and hollering. Up all night. Down-Betty ran away with—"

"The circus?" breathed Penny in awe. She regarded the old lady in the floppy hat with new respect.

"Almost, hon," laughed Down-Betty. "A crazy kind of circus called vaudeville." Then she patted the ground beside her and tossed each of them a trowel. "If you really want to hear about it, you girls should make yourselves useful."

Penny was conflicted. She didn't exactly feel like sitting and being distracted. She had things to figure out. A plan to hatch. Also, there were the raspberries to pick. But she wanted to hear this story, and besides, Luella was already sitting down.

So Penny sat down and picked up the little shovel as Betty said, "Let's see—where to begin? I went onstage for the first time at the age of eight. Trained as a juggler, then a singer. Finally I went into the air. Those were good days. Looking down on the world. Music tinkling all in my ears. Lights in my hair. And my stars, was I rolling in dough!"

Penny's ears perked up. "You *were*?"

"Seemed so at the time, anyways," said Down-Betty. "Though somehow it trickled away over the years. I'm certainly no millionaire now." She chuckled as she pulled more mint. "Not that it matters."

"But you were only *eight*?" asked Penny.

"Sure!" said Down-Betty. "When it all began, anyway. Eight is the perfect age for the stage. Nice flexible limbs.

You heal fast when you hurt yourself. You're interested in everything. Honestly, if you can't do a thing at eight, you'll have a hard time doing it later, what with all the bills and headaches and creaky bones and cumbersome marriages. Life gets too busy for *doing things* once you grow up. We grown-ups often miss out on the very best things because we're so busy being grown-ups."

Penny thought about this. "But," she asked cautiously, "didn't your parents mind? Didn't you get in trouble?"

"My parents? Ha! Mama was long gone by then— died of consumption. And Papa disappeared on a freight train when she passed away. Left me with my grand-mother. Then Gran took sick and couldn't keep me anymore, so I landed at a children's home, which was no kind of home so far as I could see. Things were bad at an orphanage in those days."

Penny had no idea what to say. This was the saddest story she'd ever heard, and it made her own problems seem small, but the way Down-Betty told the story made it sound like no big deal. The old woman tossed these facts out like confetti: light, small, colorful.

"I'm so sorry," Penny said. "I can't even imagine."

"Nope, you can't, for which you should be thankful. But don't cry for me, dearie, I've had a grand life. There's no cause to be weeping about folks long gone.

Life's too short for worry. Fix it or forget it, I always say."

"She *does* say that," confirmed Luella. "A lot. Down-Betty says *everything* a lot."

Down-Betty laughed and threw a sprig of mint at Luella. "You're a sassy thing!"

Luella stuck her tongue out.

Down-Betty continued, "You'd hardly think it to look at my scrawny chicken legs today, but in fact, I was the toast of vaudeville. I ate chocolate for breakfast and brushed my teeth with seltzer. I hung around dressing rooms listening to the old folks tell tall tales. I never saw a reason not to do just as I liked."

"No reason not to do *just as you liked?*" asked Penny.

"Sure!" said Down-Betty. "Plenty of time to be careful when you're a grown-up, right?"

Penny nodded thoughtfully. Then suddenly she set down her trowel and stood. She put her hands over her head. "Did you dance—like this?" she asked, twirling into a bed of squash.

"Almost exactly!" said Down-Betty, shaking a gloved hand in the air. "Bravo! Now *kick!*"

Penny kicked, and it felt good to stretch. She kicked again. She kicked higher. She kicked the other leg. She didn't even notice that Luella was staring at her. She closed her eyes and did just as she liked. She leaped and

spun and climbed up onto a wall to jump off. She found that the higher she kicked the higher she wanted to kick. She danced and danced, and when she was done, she lay panting in the dirt. It felt very good, like she'd let out all her worries.

"Oh, now you're reminding me so much of your aunt, I might cry," said Down-Betty. "You dance with a smile, just like she did when she was your age. Now, *there* was a character."

Penny propped herself up on her elbows. "You knew Aunt Betty all the way back when you were kids?"

"Of course! That's where we met. Onstage in a town near here, Chattanooga. I was working a place called the Liberty Theater, a nice place, as I recall. I sprained an ankle turning a pirouette, and your aunt was in the audience. Why, she hopped right up onstage and took over for me. Midspin. Improvised the whole darn thing."

"You've never told me *that* part," said Luella.

"*You* never asked," said Down-Betty. She looked at Penny and went on. "From that day forth we were inseparable. She ran away and joined up with us that very night, and we toured together. Understudied each other. When vaudeville died, the two of us took a train out to California and made movies instead. Though neither of us ever became famous—I was too homely, and Betty got too plump. But oh, we had fun." Down-Betty appeared to be lost in the past. She stroked the bunch of mint in her hand and sniffed it deeply.

"It sounds great," said Luella.

"Of course," continued Down-Betty, "it was, but *these* are the days too. Just different. I love this, sitting here smelling the earth and the herbs. The sun warm on my shoulders and birds in the sky above me. Betty and I spent a lot of years happy like *this* too."

"What else do you remember about her?" asked Penny.

"Oh, what *don't* I remember? Funny how, as I get older, I start forgetting to do the dishes and I misplace my false teeth, but I remember all the long-ago stories clear like water. I remember Betty leaving the movies to marry Fred. Though she never took his name. Hoo boy, was Fred steamed at that! There they were, just married, and they walked into the reception hall at a posh hotel in Los Angeles, all ready to make their grand entrance, and some fancy man called out, 'Presenting Mr. and Mrs. Frederick Dingler,' all official-like, and your auntie threw her hand up in the air and stomped her foot and yelled, 'I'll no sooner be a Dingler than a dingbat! I'm Betty Dewberry, pal.' And was she ever! Your aunt always did say just exactly whatever popped into her head."

Down-Betty laughed and wiped a tear from her eye, remembering. "But poor old Fred got over it."

Penny thought about this. "Then what happened?" she asked.

"Oh, then Betty and Fred left California, hit the road."

"And that's when she came here?" asked Luella.

"Not right at first," said Betty. "They traveled a lot. The Far East and down in old Mexico. They dug for treasure in Cairo, Egypt, which is where they made most of their money. We lost track of one another, as people do, but every year she'd call on my birthday."

"Treasure?" asked Penny, looking at her spade. "Really?"

"Sure," said Betty. "She used to say it was the *only* thing to dig for, treasure. She wasn't much for gardening herself. But then one day they came back here, opened up the old house, and settled down. Betty was mayor for a time. Fred taught school. Just regular everyday living, you know."

Penny had fallen silent and was digging in the ground thoughtfully.

"What about you?" asked Luella. "What did *you* do all that time?"

Down-Betty got a faraway look in her eyes. "Oh, I

danced mostly, and sang a little. I left California too and moved to Pennsylvania. To dance at a little mountain resort in feathers and paste jewels. Finally I got old and the resorts closed, so I landed in Baltimore, Maryland. For a time I worked in a deli there, a place called Attman's, where the sandwiches were as big as your head. Then one day I got my yearly call from Betty. She said Fred had passed away, and she wondered if I might like to come for a visit. The visit turned into a year, and before I knew it, I was living here at the Whippoor-willows."

Penny heard her name echoing through the garden from a distance. "Peeeeeeeeeeeeenny Grey! Where are yooooooooooooooou?" It was Dirk.

Penny tossed her spade aside and stood up quickly.

"Oh, nuts! It sounds like your dad wants those berries," said Luella.

"Yeah," said Penny. "We'd better get going."

Down-Betty smiled. "You'll find the best ones at the far end of the thicket." She gestured with a handful of mint. "Have fun, girls. Make a mess while you still can. Good luck!"

"Thanks for everything," said Penny. "Thanks a lot."

"Anytime, darlin'," said Down-Betty. "It's nice to

have you here. Makes me remember your aunt Betty. My, she must be beaming down on us right now, or *up*, maybe. Hard to guess where the old gal landed. She was a devil in her day." Down-Betty winked.

Then Penny hugged Down-Betty. She buried her face in the old woman's neck, which smelled like baby powder and tomato vines. Over the old woman's shoulder Penny could see that Luella looked surprised, but Penny found that she didn't care in the slightest. She did *just as she liked*. It was a good hug.

After that she headed off with Luella through the garden to pick berries. As she picked, she waited for Luella to tease her for dancing in the garden, and maybe for hugging Down-Betty. Funnily enough, Luella didn't say a word, and as time slipped by, Penny realized it really didn't matter either way.

Once the colander was full, the two girls ran back down the path and around to the front porch of the big house. Penny thumped up the steps to her apartment, holding the berries carefully with both hands. "You coming?" she asked Luella, turning on a step to look behind her.

"Nah." Luella waved, opening the door to her own apartment. "I'm not in a behaving-for-parents kind of mood right now. But I'll see you later. And I'm glad . . .

you're feeling better." She ran inside and slammed the door.

Penny, who *was* feeling better, continued up the steps and through the door and the living room, to set the berries on the kitchen table in front of her mom and dad. Dirk was staring off into space. Delia was reading over Willa's invitation but looking deflated. She was dressed very nicely, in a crisp white shirt and a pretty red skirt.

"You look nice," Penny told her mom with a smile.

"Nice maybe, but not nice enough to be a receptionist at the Farmer's Exchange." Delia let out a deep sigh, set down the invitation, and chewed a thumbnail. "I didn't get the job. It turns out you need to know all kinds of computery stuff, spreadsheets and databases. Funny, I hadn't thought about it being *that* kind of a job here in the country. Even farmers are high-tech nowadays, I guess. I don't know what we'll do. I really don't." Delia buried her head in her arms. Dirk reached out and patted her absentmindedly on the back.

An hour earlier this might have upset Penny, but now it didn't. Now, quite the contrary, it was as though the last piece of a puzzle were fitting into place with a firm little *click*. Penny knew now that her parents were out of *inner resources*. It was *her* turn.

She wrapped her arms around her mother just as she had wrapped them around Down-Betty. She gave Delia a big squeeze and kissed the top of Delia's head like she'd seen her father do.

Delia looked up at Penny and smiled.

BOOK FIVE

⟡

INNER RESOURCES

17

Turning the Knob

Unfortunately, the daylight was fading and it was dinnertime, so Penny obligingly ate her father's roast chicken and tomato salad and considered what lay in store for her tomorrow. Her mind swirled with thoughts of treasure calling to her from a quiet underground place. She barely noticed her parents' conversation, and she went to bed right after dinner to make morning come sooner.

But the next day she woke to a funny, joyful whooping noise. It was the sound of a happy Dirk. She climbed from her bed and padded into the next room. "What *is* it?" she asked, rubbing sleep from her eyes and yawning.

Dirk was dancing around the living room with the phone in his hand. "Whoop!" he whooped. "I just got a call! From The City! I'm going to be published! See, I told you! It was *nothing*, nothing at all to get a book deal. Oh,

I wish your mom would get home from work, already. Things *do* have a way of working out! I knew they would. I can't *wait* to see her face when she hears! An author! I'm about to be an author!"

"What? Huh! That's amazing, Dad," said Penny. She was happy for her father, of course she was. But Penny was also a little confused by this sudden news. She was absolutely certain her father had not written a word in days. He seemed to be doing everything *but* writing a book.

Besides that, today was the day *she'd* fix things, she just knew it! Otherwise, why had she found the book and the note from Aunt Betty? If it wasn't her job to find it, why was the treasure out there calling for her? Yet, here, now, was Dirk—with a solution of his own. How could that be?

"That's—great," Penny said. "I didn't think you'd finished the novel yet."

"Oh, well—the *novel*," scoffed Dirk. "*That* thing was never going to be any good anyway. Turns out I'm as bad at novel writing as I am at being president of a company! Somehow I just couldn't get myself to work on it. Making up stories and writing them down is *hard*. You have to think out every little detail."

Penny looked up at her dad, bewildered. "But then how—"

"I shifted gears entirely," said Dirk. "I'm doing a cookbook instead. A *cookbook!*"

"You *are?*" Penny asked. Her father *had* been proving himself skilled in the kitchen, but still—how could he have written a cookbook so quickly? He hadn't set foot inside his office for days.

"Well," confessed Dirk, "actually, your aunt Betty mostly wrote the recipes. But *I* deciphered her crazy old-fashioned handwriting, *I'm* rewriting it, and *I* thought to tell someone about it, so I should get some credit for that, right? It was just sitting there, and it still would be if it weren't for me. Also, I do love all the recipes and love making them. That counts for something, I think."

"You sent *that* to a publisher?" Penny asked, thinking that the stained pages in the kitchen hardly looked like something you'd want to send anyone.

"No, not exactly," explained Dirk. "I pitched the *idea* of it to a guy I know. A hotshot editor, a friend of my old buddy Joe. The hotshot liked it! He just about ate up the idea of *Up-Betty's Small-Town Kitchen.* He called it folksy and sweet, and he said that people would love the idea of a big-city businessman type guy giving up his job to move to the country and cook. He said it would be a good angle for publicity. So we've been chatting for the last day or two, and this morning he called to say that everyone was on board! Isn't that great?"

"Oh," said Penny through a disappointed smile. "Yeah. Of course it is. Congratulations. Now I guess Mother can stop worrying about the money and the house. I guess—"

Dirk held up his hand. "Well, now . . . wait a minute. Hold your horses. Let's slooow down here. We don't want to get ahead of ourselves. I mean, this is a great thing, but there's still a lot to do. The guy *definitely* wants the book, probably, but I'll need to rewrite a lot of it and update the recipes and write an introduction. Betty was very fond of lard and heavy cream, so I'll need to try out all the new recipes, and then the book will need to be laid out, and there's cover art to consider. Plus, the contract alone could take a few months."

"Really?" Penny tried not to grin. It sounded like there was still an awful lot of work to be done. "Months?" she asked.

Dirk continued. "Yes, and I suppose I also need to get your mother's permission first. After all, *she's* the one who technically inherited the recipes, along with the house. Hmm . . . Do you think she'll want credit for that? Maybe we should do this as a husband-and-wife team. That'd be an angle too. Ooh! That might be even better. . . .''

"But," said Penny, "we don't *have* months, Daddy. If we want to stay in the house, we need money now! *Someone* needs to do something now."

"Hey," said her dad, pouting. "Give a guy a break. I'm doing the best I can. These things don't happen overnight, you know."

"No, I know, I know," said Penny with a nod. "It's great news, it is. I just—we *still* need a plan, don't we?" As Penny spoke these words, she felt her sense of purpose return and swell. Just like in a book, the parts of the story kept arranging and rearranging. Her story was leading her to the caves. She knew it.

At that moment they heard Dijon puttering into the drive. Dirk's face lit up again. "Ooh! Your mom! I can't wait to tell her about the book!"

Penny headed for her room to dress quickly, and her dad dashed to the door. "Delia, Delia!" he called out. "I've hit the jackpot! Struck gold! *Gold!* Huzzah!"

Standing by her window, watching through the pink curtains as Delia climbed the steps, Penny heard these words and knew they were yet another sign. Today was her day.

"Gold," she repeated thoughtfully, walking over to her desk. She reached into the drawer and took out the note Aunt Betty had left her.

A door will only open for one who turns the knob.

She folded the note in half and slipped it into her pocket. There was no time to lose. She was ready.

Five minutes later she was passing her mom on the stairs with hardly a quick hello. Then she was pounding on Luella's door.

"Luella! Luella!" called Penny as she pounded.

"What's all the fuss?" asked Luella, opening the door. Her hair was particularly poufy today, standing all around her head in a giant circle. She touched the pouf gingerly. "Do *not* say a word," she cautioned. "My mom is trying to get out some tangles, and it hurts."

"Come *on!*" said Penny urgently. "Let's go!"

"Where?" asked Luella crankily. "Why? What's the hurry? Didn't you just hear me say I'm busy?"

"You *can't* be," said Penny. "I need you to show me the way. To the caves!"

"Can't," said Luella. "Stupid hair! We'll go another day."

Penny frowned. Fate was being unwieldy. "Well, can you maybe just tell me where they are, then, the caves?"

"*You're* going to go *alone?*" asked Luella.

"It's important," said Penny. "Urgent, even."

"Hmm," said Luella, weighing her options. "Hang on.

I just need to grab my spelunking tools." She returned a second later with a ball cap on her head and a flashlight in her hand. She was wearing a large spool of clear string like a bracelet. "Let's go," she said. "But my mom will yell at me when she realizes I'm gone, so you'll owe me. Should we get Duncan?"

Penny nodded. "Jasper too. We need a real search party!"

Luella raised an eyebrow. "You're on a mission today, aren't you?"

Penny nodded again but said no more. A mission was exactly what this was.

Duncan was allowed to come on the hunt, but only on the condition that he took along a first aid kit, a cell phone, a backup flashlight, and a bottle of water. Luella rolled her eyes at his full backpack, but it wasn't long before she had to admit that the cell phone came in handy. Halfway to town Duncan thought to call Jasper and tell her to meet them on Main Street so that they didn't have to walk all the way down her long dirt road.

Jasper joined them at the General Store, where her grandfather generously supplied them all with bubble gum. Then they set out in pairs down Main Street, chewing happily and blowing bubbles. Double file down the sidewalk, Luella and Jasper walked in front, and Penny and Duncan followed behind.

"Hey," Luella called out as she tromped along in the lead. "This is awesome. With four of us hunting, we can split up and cover more ground than I've ever explored before. Maybe today we'll really find it."

Under her breath Penny added, "We will. We *have* to."

The four kids plodded on a little farther, until suddenly Duncan stopped walking and said, "*Man,* I can't believe we didn't bring Alice along. She has the best eyesight of anyone I've ever met. She's a great thing-finder, and her summer camp finally ended yesterday."

"Oh, I forgot!" said Luella. "That *is* too bad. I hope she doesn't feel left out."

Jasper nodded without turning her head. Her long braid jumped up and down.

"Who's Alice?" asked Penny, walking quickly to keep up.

"Another kid who lives at the Whippoorwillows," answered Duncan. "She hasn't been around much since you've been here because she goes to a special camp for a week every summer. She lives in the orange house next to yours."

"Oh," said Penny as her jaw tightened strangely. It seemed forever ago that she'd embarrassed herself trying to make friends, though it had really been less than two weeks. It was funny how different Penny felt now. "Yeah," she said. "Yeah, I think I know who you mean. She has . . . um, very shiny hair."

"That's her," said Duncan.

"I met her," said Penny softly, thinking how unfair it was that the memory of a mean girl was interfering with her day. Under her breath she added, "I almost forgot about *that* girl."

Luella's ears were sharp. She spun around and looked at Penny. "What do you mean by '*that* girl'?"

The others stopped too.

"Um," said Penny, looking down at her feet, "nothing, really. I just—I don't even really know her. Never mind."

But Luella wouldn't let it drop. "Look, Penny, you're our friend and all. But you can't be mean to Alice. Nobody can. Not even me. It's a rule around here."

Luella sure knew a lot of rules, thought Penny, irritated. "*Me* mean to *her*?" she said. "*She* was mean to *me*! I *tried* to make friends. Practically begged her. She just acted like I wasn't even there, turned her shiny head, and walked the other way."

The others were silent for a minute, staring at Penny. So Penny added, "She just seemed mean."

"Probably," offered Jasper in a soft voice, "probably Alice didn't *hear* you."

Penny shook her head emphatically. "That's not possible," she said. "I *yelled* after her. Really. *You* remember." She looked at Luella. "You heard me all the way inside the house."

"Is *that* what you were doing that day? Sheesh. I wish I'd known. Penny, there's no such thing as too loud," said Luella matter-of-factly. "Not with Alice."

"What do you mean?" asked Penny gruffly, kicking at a clump of weeds.

"Because there's no such thing as loud at all when you're *deaf*," said Luella.

"What?" Penny gulped. "Huh?"

"Alice is deaf, Penny," said Duncan. "Since birth. She can't hear a word you say. You have to stare straight at her when you talk so she can read your lips."

Playing back the memory of her encounter with the girl, Penny wanted to sink into the ground. She vaguely remembered the girl looking for something at her feet, then picking up a fallen flower. If she hadn't *heard* Penny, maybe she'd just turned around at that moment by chance. Was that possible?

"Oh, gosh," said Penny.

"Yeah, *gosh*," said Luella.

Penny didn't know what to say. She groaned. "I'm an idiot," she said.

"Sometimes," said Luella. "But Alice will understand. She's used to *idiots*. She's also used to . . ." Then Luella said something else, something with her hands, something Penny didn't understand at all.

"What's that?" Penny asked.

"Sign language, of course," said Luella.

"What's it *mean*?" asked Penny.

Luella laughed. "Ha! If you want to know, I guess you'll have to ask Alice!"

Then she turned around and began walking again, like it was no big deal. Jasper and Duncan did the same. Penny gratefully followed her friends, thinking that whatever name Luella had just called her, she probably deserved.

Anyway, she didn't have time to worry about it. She had a treasure to find!

18

DARK IN THE DEEP

Walking quickly, the four friends turned off Main Street and onto a twisty mountain road. They walked in a single line up the narrow shoulder. It was scary, walking along the road like that, but it wasn't long before Luella suddenly turned to face the guardrail on her right and climbed over it. Then, from where Penny was standing, she appeared to walk straight off the cliff, with Jasper close behind her.

Penny and Duncan leaned over the guardrail to peer after the two girls. They found them crouched, sliding on their bottoms down a very steep hill. Penny and Duncan looked at each other nervously, took a deep breath, and did the same, carefully. They stepped over the metal rail and then slid, with pebbles and dirt scattering beneath them, down into a kind of ravine full of very tall trees. At the bottom was a creek bed, where only the merest trickle

of water still ran. Luella led the way along the trickle, past boulders, rusted tin cans, a broken lawn chair, and a moldy duffel bag, beneath a web of leafy green braches and dappled sunlight.

Finally they came to the mouth of a cave. The cave was a black hole cut into the side of the mountain, a gaping yawn. Just above the cave someone had spray-painted the words NO ENTRY.

Standing by the opening, Penny shivered. The air that came from the cave's mouth was cool. She could see nothing past the mouth of the cave. Luella turned on her flashlight and pointed it into the dim. The cave was so enormous, so cavernous, so huge, that the flashlight beam hardly made a dent in the darkness. Who knew what lurked in there?

"You all ready?" Luella asked as she tied the end of her string around a tree that stood at the cave's mouth.

Penny, who only an hour before had been absolutely certain that the solution to everything waited inside this cave, now felt unsure.

"How will we ever find *anything* in there?" asked Jasper. "It's so dark."

"That's what makes it a treasure *hunt*," explained Luella. "If the treasure were hanging out in a nice, dry, little cave next to a big sign that said TREASURE, it wouldn't still *be* there, would it? Somebody else would have found it long before us."

Penny stared timidly into the pitch-black of the cave. She turned on her flashlight, and Jasper and Duncan followed suit. Three more beams of light met the first and roved around the cave walls like searchlights. When the kids all pointed their beams directly ahead at the cave's floor about twenty feet in, they saw a plank of wood.

"What's that wood for?" asked Duncan.

"That's a bridge," said Luella. "It's to keep you from falling into the gully."

"Gully?" whispered Jasper.

"Well," qualified Luella, "I don't know if it's *technically* a gully, but it's a big hole in the ground."

"How big a hole?" asked Duncan. "I mean, if I fell into it, would I . . . make it?"

"What's *in* the gully?" asked Penny.

"Oh, come *on*!" cried Luella. "You guys are a pack of sissies. *Yes*, there is a gully, and *yes*, it is deep and scary, and *yes*, it is very dark in the cave, and *yes*, there might even be animals inside it. How do I know? I don't check with all the animals in the woods, find out their schedules! This is *supposed* to be a treasure hunt, not a tea party!" With that, Luella tromped off into the darkness, her flashlight beam trained on the cave floor just ahead of her. When her feet hit the plank of wood, Penny could hear a different kind of thud. The clear string unspooled behind her with a whisper. It was very thin string.

The others looked at each other and then pointed their flashlights in Luella's direction, but she had gone too far into the cave to see much besides a little blur of light. This was not reassuring.

"Come ON—ON—ON—ON!" echoed Luella's voice, bouncing against the cave walls insistently. Penny, Duncan, and Jasper stared at each other.

"You first," said Duncan, nudging Penny. "This was *your* idea."

It *was* her idea, and she did want to find the treasure. She *needed* to find the treasure. With a huge breath, Penny stepped after her friend into the cave, staring at the spot of cave floor illuminated by her flashlight beam. Gently, she touched the taut piece of clear plastic string that connected her to Luella ahead. When she reached the shivery, shaky plank of wood, she tiptoed onto it, trying just to stare at her feet and not to think about what lay beneath it in the gully. She wanted to hang on to the piece of string, but she didn't, for fear it would snap.

Penny could feel how enormous the drafty space around her was. It was chilly and smelled like a basement, or maybe like rain. She stopped for a second and pointed her flashlight directly above her, but the ceiling was so high that the spot of light disappeared before it could find the stone roof of the cave. Penny pointed the light back at her feet and stared again at the only spot she could make out in the dark, the white-yellow spot of light traveling six inches ahead of her feet, the speck of light that illuminated the filthy plank of wood. Above her she heard a small scratchy sound, and then a rustle and a flapping of wings. Something brushed past her in the dark, and she gasped, teetered, wobbled, and almost fell.

"Lu?" she called out in a tiny voice. No answer.

"Luella? Are you there?" Her voice echoed endlessly. Penny reached out wildly for the plastic string again but couldn't find it.

Then Luella's voice came back, warm and friendly, from just a few feet ahead. "You're doing great! Come on, Penny!"

Penny pointed her flashlight directly in front of her at waist level and caught a glimpse of blue denim.

"You only need to walk about ten feet, and then there's solid ground," said Luella. "I promise."

"Okay," said Penny. "I can do that."

Behind her Penny could feel Duncan and Jasper stepping onto the plank. Each time more weight was added,

the plank bounced slightly. Penny felt frozen, but she forced herself to inch along. Because she *knew* what waited for her on the other side was Luella—and the treasure. She minced forward, her arms rigid in front of her, clutching the flashlight, until suddenly the spot of light before her revealed a dirty stone floor. Penny sprang forward. She thought she'd never been as happy as she was the minute she felt her feet on the reassuring stone surface of the cave floor. She wanted to lie down on it and kiss it.

In the darkness Luella's hand found Penny's arm. They lit each other's faces up and both grinned.

"I did it!" said Penny.

"You sure did," answered Luella. "And look, here's Duncan!" She pointed her flashlight at where Duncan was stepping off the plank.

Penny heard a thump, which was Duncan sitting down on the ground immediately.

When he spoke, he sounded relieved and overwhelmed. "W-w-wow," he said. "Let's not tell my parents about this."

Jasper followed, hopping off the plank and hitting the stone floor with a small thud.

"Gosh, Luella," she called out. "You really do this alone, all by yourself? What if you fell into the gully?"

Luella snickered.

"What?" asked Duncan. "What's so funny?"

Luella laughed louder.

"What *is* it?" asked Penny, mildly exasperated.

"I lied," said Luella with a snort. "That *gully* is only a ditch about a foot deep. I dragged the plank there myself one time when it was full of gross water and leaves and my shoes got all wet. I just wanted to see if you guys were chicken. The good news is you aren't!"

"Hey!" said Duncan. "Hey, that's mean. I was really scared."

"That really wasn't very nice, Luella," said Jasper.

But Penny found she was strangely grateful to Luella

for the fib. She didn't *tell* her friend that, because she didn't think Luella needed to be rewarded for her tricks, and Jasper and Duncan seemed genuinely upset. Still, Penny felt good about what she'd just done, extremely good. So what if it wasn't really a dangerous gully and a narrow, teetery bridge? It *had* been for a few minutes, as far as Penny was concerned.

Penny smiled in the darkness. With nobody to see her joy, she felt her face split open in a goofy grin. Then she stuck her tongue out and flailed her arms, taking full advantage of the invisibility. It felt good.

"Okay, so now what?" asked Duncan, standing up and brushing off the seat of his jeans. He aimed his flashlight at Luella.

"Over here," she said, patting the wall beside her. "Follow me along this wall, until you come to an opening."

They all followed in the dark, with the thin light from their flashlights bouncing along and their hands flat against the wall, until they found the opening. Then they stepped into a much smaller passage. It was long and narrow, and together their four flashlights were enough to cast a dim yellow light evenly throughout the room. The four kids blinked happily, surprised and delighted to see each other's smudgy faces. The inside of the cave looked how Penny imagined the inside of a dripped sand castle, all brown and gray and full of stalagmites and stalactites. The walls were wet. There were tunnels leading off in different directions.

"Ooh!" said Penny, glancing around at the shadows and shapes.

"This is *much* better," said Jasper.

"Yeah," said Luella. "Almost all the caves are skinny like this once you get past that one big room. Some are really just little tunnels."

"So," said Penny, looking at Luella. "*Now* what? Where do we start?"

"You tell me," said Luella. "I got us here, but you're the one who's so sure we're going to find the treasure today. I've been looking for years and haven't had any luck yet. What's *your* plan?"

"Oh," said Penny. "I don't know. Let me think."

In Penny's imagination, the plan had simply been to *find* the treasure. She had envisioned herself stumbling upon the treasure chest and opening it with a creak to reveal a wealth of gold bars and nuggets and coins. She had imagined arriving home with her pockets and hands full of riches, but that was as far as she'd gotten with her plan. She had figured out *what* was supposed to happen, just not *how* it would happen. Penny hadn't given much thought to the details of the search itself.

So now Penny closed her eyes and felt for an answer. She put her hand in her pocket, touched the note, and said silently, *I wish I knew what to do. I wish there would be a sign.*

Penny waited. No sign.

She tried again, whispering this time, barely mouthing the words. *"Just a tiny sign? Anything at all?"*

Penny searched for a doorknob to turn, and this time something happened. Somewhere down the long, dark tunnel, there was a sound. The sound was so small that nobody else even heard it. It was the sound of a small stick breaking, or the sound of a pebble falling. It was the faint echo of a sound. But Penny heard it.

"This way!" she called, opening her eyes and ducking into a passageway.

The others followed close behind.

19

A Way Out

Penny and Luella and Jasper and Duncan walked. They walked and hunted, and their invisible spelunking thread unspooled beside them. Their flashlights scoped the ground at their feet and bounced off the walls, and at last Penny and her friends found themselves at a fork, a place where the tunnel split evenly in two. To the left there was a small narrow tunnel that led slightly down, and to the right, a wider tunnel that led slightly up.

"Down!" said Penny, heading to the left.

Duncan stopped. "No," he said. "I think we should go this way." He pointed to the larger tunnel. "Down seems too . . . I don't know, *down*."

But now Penny could feel the pull of the treasure and knew they needed to go down. She was certain of this, or nearly certain, anyway. "No," she said, "I'm going *this* way. The treasure is over here."

"Suit yourself," said Duncan a little grouchily. "But I'm tired of doing what people tell me to do. I'm going this way. We can meet back here in about an hour. Okay?"

"Okay," said Penny. "I guess."

"I don't know," said Jasper. "We're already pretty deep into the caves, and we only have one spool of fishing line. Should we really separate?"

But Penny and Duncan were already heading off in their different directions.

"You keep an eye on that knucklehead!" Luella called to Jasper. "Don't let him go far. Keep track of your turns, and come back after the tunnel splits three times. I'll watch out for this one." Luella followed after Penny.

Deep in her tunnel, with Luella behind her, Penny began to sing to herself. She didn't like that Duncan and Jasper had gone the other way. It scared her a little, and singing made her less nervous. "*Somewhere over the rainbow . . . ,*" she sang.

When Luella heard her, she joined in at the top of her lungs. "*Way up hiiiiiiiiiiiiiiiiigh!*"

Elsewhere, off in the cave, Penny could hear Duncan and Jasper singing too. Which made it feel like they were all still together, kind of. Nobody could be *too* terribly lost if you could hear them. Could they?

As the minutes ticked by, Penny felt less convinced she had made the right decision. Her fingers felt for holes and niches in the walls, and she scattered piles of rocks on the floor, hunting beneath them for a secret hiding spot. At one point Luella found a yellowish length of tarnished chain, which may or may not have been real gold, but was by no means Blackrabbit's treasure. Once she stopped singing, she could hear the faint hiss of the fishing line unwinding.

"Luella," she said finally, stopping. "Do you think we'll find the treasure?"

"Eh, who knows?" said Luella. "But does it matter? Aren't you having fun? What's the big deal?"

"The big deal is . . . ," began Penny. "Nothing."

Penny *wanted* to tell her friend. She wanted to, but she couldn't. Explaining that her parents needed money was one thing, but *this* was so complicated. How could she tell Luella that if the bank took the house away, all the tenants of the Whippoorwillows might lose their homes?

"No big deal," she said instead.

"Well, it *seems* like it is," said Luella in the darkness. "And also, why are you so sure we'll find it today? You're weird."

Penny didn't know how to tell her friend about her wishes or the signs. She wasn't ready to show Luella the note in her pocket. If she did, she would sound even weirder. "No reason," she said as she continued to hunt. The farther she went and the deeper into the cave she got, the less certain she became. Both girls slowed down. Eventually Luella sat down to rest. "I *think*," she said, patting the ground beside her, "we might need to call it a day and go swimming. I'm hot and I have dirt in my nose. Besides, Jasper and Duncan don't have any fishing line. We should go meet back up with them. Come on!"

Across the room Penny was pulling and tugging at a stubborn boulder.

"Give it a rest, Penny," said Luella. "We can come back anytime."

"No," said Penny. "We *can't*. You don't understand. Plus, I think I might have it. I think this might be it. If I can just—just—oof!" She tugged harder, trying to roll the boulder away from the wall, where there was a cubby-hole of sorts, blocked by the boulder.

Luella rolled her eyes. "Penny, you are *never* going to move that boulder."

"I have to," said Penny. "I will. I'm going to find that treasure if it kills me."

"Whatever," said Luella.

"No, *not* whatever!" cried Penny, tugging and straining and—just then the rock shuddered and moved. It slid aside, rolled slightly, and revealed the cubbyhole behind it to be a tunnel. A small black hole in the rock wall. Penny pointed her flashlight and stared. "Hey, look," she said. "Look at this, Luella!"

Luella got up and walked over. They peered through the narrow hole and into a tunnel together. "Well, would you look at *that*," Luella said as Penny stuck a leg into the hole, then crouched down to wiggle the rest of her body inside it.

Penny disappeared into the hole as Luella shouted, "Hey, wait for me!" But Luella would not fit! She was only a few inches taller than Penny, but she was also a good bit sturdier, and no matter how she wiggled, she couldn't get more than a leg or arm through the hole.

"Penny," she called out. "Come back here! You don't know what you're doing. You don't have any fishing line! We shouldn't all be splitting up! This makes me nervous. Hey! *Listen* to me!"

Penny turned around and called back behind her, "If you were me right now, would *you* come back? Would *you* listen?"

It took Luella a second to answer. "Well, no," she said. "Probably not. But *I* don't listen to anyone. Just ask my mom."

So Penny turned around and headed off down the

tunnel. She was determined, and she was certain again—and then she was gone. The last thing she heard was Luella yelling after her, "I swear, Penny Grey, if you don't come back this minute, I'm leaving you here and going home! I'm going swimming! *SWIMMING!* Without *you!*"

Penny ignored her friend and headed off bravely, but once she was inside the tunnel, she felt less brave. She could tell that nobody had been there in a long time. The air was musty and still. Her flashlight filled the small space with dim light, but she almost wished it didn't, because there were some bones in one spot—bones that could have belonged to anything, or anyone. She saw a shoe in another place, a very old-looking boot. Penny wondered if it was possible that the boot belonged to a dead miner. Behind her Penny could hear Luella calling out her name, but she just kept walking.

About fifty feet in, Penny came to a deep recess in the ground. The hole ran from one side of the tunnel to the other, so there was no way around it. Penny sized up the hole, which she thought was about five feet wide, and decided that if she took a running start, she could probably clear it. But what if she didn't?

She pointed her flashlight down into the hole and discovered that she could see the bottom. It looked forgotten and covered in dirt. When she directed her flashlight ahead of her, down the tunnel and past the hole, she saw nothing but more tunnel. *Surely there must be something there,* Penny thought. This tunnel was too well hidden, too carefully blocked, to be an accident. Pointing her flashlight beam behind her at the old boot, she thought, *Somebody was here, long ago, and sealed this place up on purpose. Why would they bother to do such a thing unless they were protecting something . . . a secret. . . . And why, if I wasn't supposed to find the treasure, would I have found this passage? My wishes brought me here. It's not just an accident. I can do this. I have to do this. In a book I would do this.*

As Penny saw things, she had only two choices. She could take a chance, keep going, and find the treasure, or she could admit defeat, rejoin her friends, and wait for her parents to tell her to pack her boxes again.

There was no choice.

Penny walked back down the tunnel a little ways, crossed her fingers, aimed her flashlight, took a running start, and then leaped.

For a moment she was airborn! She was flying through the dank air of the cave, holding her breath, waiting for ground to rise and meet her on the other side of the hole.

Then she plummeted.

Penny landed in the hole with the wind knocked out of her. When she took a deep breath, she sucked in dust. She coughed and choked but found herself surprisingly unhurt. She'd lost her flashlight in the fall, so everything around her was dark. Penny rooted through the dirt and rotting cloth beneath her and quickly found the light again. Then she looked around and gasped!

She was in a tiny makeshift room, which was wider than the top of the hole. The pile of old blankets she'd landed in were brown and rotting to dust, but they were made up to be a little bed, complete with a thin pillow. She shined her flashlight to her left and found that on the dirty rock floor was a pile of rusty cans, an opener, and a fork. BEANS, said one can. SWEETENED CONDENSED MILK, said another. Some mice or rats had made a home from a paper sack that sat beside the cans. Penny shivered and turned her light away from the nest. To her right she found a pile of neatly folded, moth-eaten clothes, all of them the same color—a shade halfway between gray and brown. The clothes sat on an old wooden box, about the size of a peach crate, with rusty handles at each end. Beside the clothes were a comb and a little tin. The tin said HOBART'S HAIR BUTTER. Wedged into one handle of the box was a squashed hat. Hanging inside the other handle was a toothbrush. Beside the box was a pile of what looked like tools: a knife, a coiled rope, a hammer. Someone had been living here long ago!

Just beside the tools Penny spotted a magazine—nearly disintegrated, dark and unreadable, but she picked it up and found she could make out a picture on the front, a picture of a man riding a horse. Could it be a penny dreadful? Penny closed her eyes and took a deep breath. She let the magazine fall from her hands. In the darkness she felt like crying and laughing all at once.

When Penny opened her eyes, she forgot the magazine because something else caught her attention. Burned into the side of the wooden box, there was some writing. When Penny reached out and brushed aside the sleeve of a gray-brown shirt, she could make out the letters in the dim light.

BB.

Penny gasped.

BB!

Briscoe Blackrabbit?

She leaned forward again to look. Yes. It had to be. *This* was why she'd come to the cave, after all. *This* was what she'd been meant to find today. This was the answer to her wishes, her happy ending.

Penny nearly fell over in the dark as she rushed to push the clothes, tin, and comb to the ground. When she

tried to lift the box, she found it was heavy—very heavy. "Of *course* it's heavy," she said aloud in the darkness. "*Gold* is heavy." Grunting, Penny managed to tip the box onto its side. Something inside it clanked. Then Penny squatted beside it to take a closer look. The box was made of very thick, heavy wooden planks, and it was sealed with nails that had long ago rusted into place. Penny picked up the knife from the floor and tried to pry out a nail. The blade was old and thin, and it broke, scraping Penny's finger.

So, with her finger in her mouth, Penny stood up. She managed to lift one side of the box a few inches off the ground, but the walls of the hole were far too high for her to see over, much less heave the box over. What could she do?

Penny set the box down, then pushed it against the wall again. With a labored groan she turned it on its end so that it was taller than it was wide. When she climbed up on it, her head was only a foot below the top of the hole. She stuck her arm out of the hole, turned her flashlight back in the direction she'd come from, and began to yell.

"LUELLA!"

But Luella didn't answer. Was it possible she'd really left Penny behind and gone swimming?

"LUUUUUEEEEELLA! HEEEEEELP!"

Penny yelled for a few more minutes, but Luella never yelled back. No beam of light found its way to her. Luella really *did* seem to have deserted her.

Standing on the box on her tiptoes, Penny tried to climb out of the hole. She could get her fingers up and over the lip of the hole, but her dusty hands could find nothing to grasp. They slipped in the dust, and she fell back onto the box. By now her fingernails were torn and packed with dirt. She was bleeding where the knife had scraped her. It hurt. Frustrated, Penny climbed back down into the hole and sat on the box, her face in her hands, to think. How would she ever get the treasure home now that she had found it?

But a person can only feel frustrated for so long. After a bit Penny got angry—at Luella. *Really,* she thought, *what's the point of finding the treasure, and getting it home, and staying in Thrush Junction, if my best friend is someone who'd leave me in a dark tunnel alone? What kind of a friend is that?* She pictured the others off swimming and laughing and playing in the lake she still hadn't even seen.

After a few minutes of this fury Penny's flashlight died, and her anger made way for another emotion: fear.

In the suffocating darkness Penny heard a rustling on the floor near her feet, and she jumped up on the box with a shriek. She stood on the box, shaking a little. Now it dawned on her that she was *really* stuck in a hole. *Stuck in a hole!* Who knew how long it would be before Luella realized she hadn't come home? She could be stranded here overnight! Maybe even for days!

Penny's stomach growled. Her throat felt parched. She looked around again, but everywhere was darkness. She touched the stone walls of the hole beside her, felt how solid they were, how hard. There was no way to dig herself out.

She climbed down from the box and gingerly rooted in the clutter for the rope. At last she found it, but even with the old rope in her hands, she was lost. A rope isn't much good at the *bottom* of a hole.

So Penny did the only thing left to do. She cried. She perched on top of the box, put her head on her knees, and wept.

At first she cried because she was stuck in a hole and abandoned by her friends. But there in the dark, thoughts swarmed in her head, and she found herself thinking about her parents and their money and all the years she'd wasted being bored and sulky. When she hadn't had any problems, she'd been miserable, and now that she knew *how* to be happy, she had real problems. Like being poor. And stuck in a hole.

Penny cried and cried, and even once she'd run out of

things to cry about, she kept crying because she was alone, and she could because there was nobody to hear her.

Only there *was* someone.

"Penny?" came a voice from down the tunnel, a gentle voice. The voice was accompanied by a beam of light. "Are you okay?" The voice got closer. The light too.

It was Jasper.

Penny looked up, and her wet face split open with a smile in the light. "You're here! You came back! You didn't leave me!" she said, rubbing her dirty face with the dirty back of a hand.

"Of course not," said Jasper. "We never would. But Duncan and Luella can't fit in here, so I came by myself."

"I thought—I thought Luella said she was going swimming."

"Oh, well," laughed Jasper. "You can't listen to *Luella*. She says a lot of things. She just ran back with the fishing line to get me and Duncan."

Penny dried her eyes with her shirt, stood up on the box, and pointed excitedly at her feet. "Hey, I found something! It's a heavy box. And it says *BB* on the side. I think it must be the treasure!"

"That's great," said Jasper with a grin. "Only it won't do us much good down there. Come on!" She reached down a hand.

"Wait a minute," said Penny, disappearing into the hole and reappearing with the rope in her hand. "I have an idea."

In no time at all Penny had tied one end of the rope around a handle of the box. She passed the other end to Jasper, who managed to fix it to a sturdy stalagmite. Then Penny climbed out of the hole, holding on to the rope with one hand and Jasper's fingers with the other. She felt like an explorer scaling a wall, climbing a mountain. It was fun.

After that the two girls, with lots of grunting and heaving, pulled the box from the hole. It was dead weight, and they almost didn't manage it. Jasper wanted to give up and come back for it later, but Penny insisted. "No, we can do it! I know we can do it! It isn't that big. We *have* to do it." So together they grabbed on to the rope, and hand over hand, they tugged and strained and finally pulled the box up over the lip of the hole and into the tunnel.

Then each girl took a handle and, groaning, they carried the box back to the tunnel's tight opening, where Luella and Duncan waited for them with cheers and shouts.

"Sorry I left you," Penny said to Luella after she'd stepped out into the ring of flashlights and pulled the box through after her. "But I found the treasure, I think!

Look!" She pointed to the letters on the side of the box. "I told you I would. I *knew* I'd find it."

Luella shook her head in bewilderment and said in an unusually serious tone, "I *can't* believe it. I really can't. Jeez." She looked at Penny curiously, her head tilted slightly. "It's almost like you *knew*, like you had some kind of premonition or something."

Penny didn't know how to respond to that. "I did. Kind of . . ." That was as much as she could figure out how to say.

Then, in a brighter voice, Luella cried, "What are we waiting for? Let's see what we've got!"

As quickly as four kids can lug a heavy wooden box, the friends made their way back out of the cave, following their fishing line around each curve and turn, banging their calves on the treasure with every step and shouting excitedly about what they would do with all their gold.

"I want a boat!" said Duncan.

"Well, sure," said Luella. "Who doesn't? Boats for everyone!"

They carried their load out into the burning midday sunlight, where they all took turns beating on the box and tugging at the corners of the wooden planks. Duncan found a rusty bottle opener in the creek bed and tried to pry the box open with that, but it was no use.

At last Penny stood back, wiped a slick of sweat from her forehead, and said, "I think we just have to carry it home nailed shut like this. We'll never get it open here."

"Yeah," said Luella. "What we need is a *sledgehammer.*"

"Maybe *first* we can try a crowbar?" suggested Jasper. "Or the back end of a hammer?"

"Anyway," added Duncan, "if we have to carry it home, I'm sure glad it has handles." He reached for one end of the box.

They heaved the box of treasure along the little creek and pushed it up the hill to the twisty road. They carried it home along the shoulder. Taking turns, and blistering their hands terribly, they lugged the box slowly, all the while aware of the mysterious clanking and clinking sounds coming from within. Finally they got it back to the Whippoorwillows.

Once the box was safely on the porch, Luella ran to fetch a crowbar from Down-Betty's utility shed. She handed it to Penny, saying, "Here you go, treasure seeker. Show us what you found!"

Penny stared at Luella. Then she stared at the sky. "Thank you," she said under her breath, to nobody in particular.

At last Penny turned to the box. She attacked it with a ferocity that shocked everyone. She pried and pulled and splintered the wood with the crowbar. She clobbered the top of the box and split off chunks of wood. She probably took longer and made more noise than she needed to, but her friends just stepped back and let her go at it. Finally one of the side panels came loose from the box and fell off. Penny stopped, crowbar aloft, and stared at the gleam of something inside the box. When the sunlight caught the contents of the box, it shone!

Everyone held their breath. Everyone leaned over to see. Everyone waited as Penny reached out and pulled a second panel of wood loose.

Then everyone let out their breath in a disappointed gust as a dark, cloudy glass bottle rolled from the box and onto the floor of the porch with a thump.

"No!" cried Penny. "No, no, *no!*"

Nobody else spoke. They all just stared at the bottle.

Penny dropped the crowbar and said sadly, "It can't be!" She fell to her knees to look inside the box. "It can't!" She reached inside the box, slicing her arm on a jagged piece of wood as she felt for gold bars or coins or nuggets. Or anything! But no. No. Just more bottles. A box full of bottles. Horrible, dirty bottles.

Penny sat down on the warm wooden floor of the porch, beside the box, and stared at her bloody arm. She sucked on her scraped finger. Then she fell silent.

"Penny?" said Jasper. "Penny?"

Penny didn't answer.

Duncan crouched down and picked up the bottle. He wiped it clean with his shirt and examined it.

Nobody spoke.

"It said BB," said Penny at last, in a flat voice. "It said *BB*. BB is Briscoe Blackrabbit. How could it *not* be his treasure?"

"Because," said Duncan gently and cautiously, "*BB* also stands for Bastable Bourbon. See?" He held out the bottle.

Penny looked at the bottle in his hand, gleaming in the sunlight. "But I was supposed to find it," she said. "I was going to fix everything."

"What everything?" asked Jasper kindly. "What needs fixing?"

"Yeah," said Duncan, "what's going on?"

Penny heaved a sigh. She said nothing at first, but her face looked strained, almost as if she were in pain and trying not to cry.

"Penny? Are you all right?" asked Luella in a careful voice.

Penny shook her head, her lips drawn and her eyes shut. She crossed her arms over her knees and rocked.

Luella sat down next to Penny, and then hugged her. "Really, Penny. You can tell us. What's going on?"

"No, I *can't* tell you," said Penny, opening her eyes. "It's too awful."

"Sure you can," said Duncan, setting down the bottle and sitting on Penny's other side. "You can tell us anything. That's what friends *do*. They tell each other things."

Jasper sat down too, so that the four friends were sitting in a small circle beside the disappointing box.

"Spill it," said Luella. "No secrets here."

Penny looked at the three friendly, interested faces. It had not occurred to her to think of this as a *secret*. In books secrets were fun and mysterious. This didn't feel fun *or* mysterious. It just felt sad and real.

She took a deep breath and said, "I guess you'll find out soon anyway, so I might as well tell you now. . . . It's the house, the Whippoorwillows."

"What *about* the house?" asked Luella. "What on earth does finding the treasure have to do with the house?"

"Give her a chance to explain, Lu," said Jasper. "Go on, Penny. Take your time."

"Thanks," said Penny with a sigh. "It's hard because I don't even really understand just what's happened, but I guess my aunt Betty didn't have enough money when she died, and she didn't really *own* the house entirely.

The bank owns part of it because she was supposed to pay them some money. So now, since we inherited the house, we also inherited the money . . . *problems.*" She whispered the word *problems* as she looked at Luella. "But we don't *have* any money. We used to have a lot, sort of, but we don't anymore. We're . . . *poor.*"

"Oh," said Duncan. "Oh."

"Well, join the club," said Jasper. "Nearly everyone is poor in Thrush Junction, if you want to call *that* poor. My mom talks all the time about how she can't afford to fix the truck."

"Yeah. Or if you want to see *really* poor, we can walk over to the freight yards in South Junction and watch the hobos cook their dinner," added Luella. "*That's* poor."

"We aren't hobos," said Penny sadly. "But we're going to lose the house."

"Oh," said Duncan again.

"Oh," chorused Jasper and Luella.

"Yeah, *oh,*" said Penny, looking up and around at her friends. "See, it's awful. I thought we wouldn't if I could find the treasure. I thought I could find the treasure. . . ." She sucked her finger. "No, it was more than that. I *knew* I would find the treasure. Inside myself, somehow, I could just *feel* that the gold was waiting for me. There in the caves. It was like magic or something. I wished, and there were signs. Like in a book." She looked up at her friends.

Luella, Jasper, and Duncan stared back at her, but nobody said anything.

Penny's nose had begun to drip, and she wiped it with the back of her hand without even thinking twice about it. "I just—I just love Thrush Junction so much, but now we'll have to go back to The City, where my parents can get jobs, and they'll be all busy and sad again, and I'll be so lonely and miss you guys all so much!" She wiped her nose again and sniffed.

"Oh, Penny. I'm sorry," said Jasper.

Luella dug her chin into her knee and said nothing.

"What will happen to *us*," asked Duncan, "if the bank takes the house?"

Luella looked up at Penny and raised an eyebrow. "Yeah, what *will* happen to us?"

Penny took a deep breath. "I don't know," she said. "But I don't think it's good."

"Hmm," said Duncan worriedly.

"I know," said Penny. "I know. I'm so sorry."

"It's okay, Penny," said Jasper.

"Yeah, it's not *your* fault," added Duncan.

Luella stood up and brushed off the seat of her shorts. For once she had nothing to say.

20

THE END OF THE BEGINNING

The next few days were uneventful. In fact they were painfully ordinary.

Dirk tried out six different variations on Aunt Betty's recipe for chowchow and waited for his editor to call. Delia went to work each morning on the garbage truck and called to nag the real estate agent in The City every afternoon. Meanwhile, Penny pretty much disappeared into the velvet folds of the sofa, where she read and sulked and was generally unhappy. Penny didn't even *want* to be happy anymore. She didn't want to have fun because the more wonderful her life in Thrush Junction was, the harder she thought it would be to leave behind. Once, when Duncan stopped by the apartment and her father knocked on her door to get her, she pretended to be sound asleep.

But there was another reason Penny was unhappy:

ever since they'd found the box of bottles in the cave, Luella had been absent. She hadn't stopped by and she hadn't answered her door. Penny was trying not to think about that.

Time passed slowly.

Then, when Sunday morning arrived, Penny opened her eyes very early and could not go back to sleep. The clock said it was not yet six. After rolling over four times, she finally climbed out of bed and headed into the kitchen for a glass of water. The sky outside the window was still a dusky gray.

In the kitchen Penny found her parents already up, deep in conversation. The room smelled like coffee and toast.

"Why are you up so early?" she asked.

Neither Dirk nor Delia answered. They just stared at her apologetically over the rims of their mugs.

"*What?*" she asked. But Penny knew the answer. "Go ahead," she murmured. "Just get it over with. Say it. We're moving, aren't we?"

Delia nodded slowly.

"When?" asked Penny.

"Tomorrow if at all possible," answered her father sadly. "Sorry, kiddo." Then he stared over Penny's shoulder through the open window. "Wow!" he said.

Penny turned around and saw why. Through the trees the sun was suddenly pushing its way up into the gray sky. Fingers of pink and orange and gold light were creeping over the mountains and through the dark branches and leaves so that all the trees looked as if they'd been set on fire. It was the most beautiful thing Penny had ever seen, and she forgot the awfulness entirely for a moment.

In under five minutes it was over, leaving behind another fine morning in Thrush Junction. The trees were green and the sun was up, burning its usual yellow in the sky.

Penny turned back around. "Everything changed so fast," she said.

"Yes, *everything* did," agreed Delia. Her eyes were wet, but smiling.

Penny looked from her mother to her father. "Why do we have to go so *soon?*" she asked.

Delia sighed. "It just seems like a good idea to leave before someone from the bank shows up to kick us out."

"We've done all we can," said Dirk. "But we're out of ideas."

Delia nodded. "And though I'm sure it would be a month or so before anyone would actually evict us, I don't think we want to wait and see what *that's* like."

Then Delia set down her mug and laid her hands in an odd way on her belly. "Plus," she added, "there are some other reasons—*good* reasons—to get ourselves settled sooner rather than later."

"I—I understand," said Penny hesitantly, but she didn't really, not quite. She looked curiously at her mother, who wore a strange, calm smile.

"Hey, and we still have the potluck tonight!" Dirk tried to sound cheerful. "That's fun, right?"

Penny frowned at her father. "I'm not in the mood for fun."

"Penny," added her mother softly, "I promise, it won't be so horrible in The City. It won't be like before. Things will be different now."

"What do you mean, *different?*" asked Penny. "How can you know that?"

Delia smiled and moved one of her hands from her belly, reaching out to stroke Penny's hair. "I mean they'll be better," she said. "How could they not be? *We're* different."

Penny thought about this. It was true.

Delia sighed and looked out the window. "We'll take that with us wherever we go. I'll find work, and . . . and your dad will finish his cookbook. We'll go ahead and sell the house in The City, I think, and rent a nice apartment for a while. We'll find you a real school where you can make friends. Everything will be different. Okay?"

Penny nodded, thinking it might not be too horrible. Still, it felt like a wholesome, boring lesson at the end of the worst kind of book. Penny turned to leave the room. "I have to go pack," she said dismally. "Tomorrow is *soon*."

"Okay," said Delia, "but before you go, dear, there's just one more thing. . . ."

Penny stopped walking, but she didn't turn around. "What is it now?" she asked with her back to her parents.

"I just think," said Delia, "that we'll all be pretty busy, and distracted, what with the new baby. And I hope I can count on your help. . . ."

It took a moment for these words to sink in. Then Penny whirled around. "New *baby*?" she cried.

Dirk burst out laughing, but the look on Delia's face was soft, quietly excited. She nodded simply. Her smile glowed.

Penny flew into her mother's arms. "A *sister*!"

"Well," Delia said into Penny's hair, "I suppose it *could* be a brother. But that wouldn't be *so* awful, would it?"

That evening, after an overwhelming day of baby dreams and painful packing, Penny walked with her parents slowly along the garden path behind the house.

Willa had drawn a little map on their invitation, but it wasn't really necessary, as the path was straight and true. It led away from the back of the Whippoorwillows, past the garden where Penny had danced with Down-Betty and gwowled with Twent, past the raspberry thicket, and past the woods—that tangle of trees and vines where she and Luella had gathered branches for their fort. When the woods ended, the path cut across a large clearing, at the end of which the Greys spotted a gazebo and some tables beside a lake. The tables were lit up with torches and surrounded by people. As they walked across the clearing, they heard music.

Penny stopped walking and stared. She almost didn't want to be there. It was too hard to see her friends, knowing that she'd be leaving so soon. She felt jittery about not having seen Luella for days, and nervous about why that was. But the news of the baby was burning inside her, and she couldn't wait to tell the others. *Besides*, she told herself, *I'm leaving. I can't go away without saying goodbye.*

As she neared the gazebo, she took a deep breath. The air smelled like honeysuckle and citronella, and the tables groaned with food. Penny's friends were sitting in a circle with paper plates on the lawn. She waved and ran over.

"Hi," she said to Luella, feeling shy.

Luella was her usual snarky self. "Hey, stranger," she said. "What are you waiting for? Grab a plate before all the good stuff is gone and you have to eat my mom's mushroom-tofu scramble." Luella made an *ew* face.

Penny laughed and made a face back. This would be just fine. Luella wasn't mad.

Then Penny headed over to the food tables, where she fixed herself a plateful of shish kebabs, deviled eggs, three-bean salad and twice-baked potatoes. She found a spot on the grass between Luella and Duncan. Jasper had come to the picnic too, and was spending the night with Luella and Alice, who was sitting across from Penny in the small circle, beside Twent.

"You can sleep over too," said Luella. "Of course. Or we can come up to *your* place if you want us to." She looked from Alice to Jasper and added, "Her dad makes the *best* breakfasts!"

Penny noticed that when she spoke to Alice, Luella looked straight at her and spoke very clearly. So Penny tried to do the same. "Hi, Alice," she said carefully. "I've heard a lot of nice things about you." Penny blushed and hoped it was dusky enough that nobody could tell.

But Alice just laughed with her mouth full of hamburger and said, "You too, Penny!" Her voice sounded exotic to Penny, almost like she had a foreign accent. *Her voice is curvy,* Penny thought, *soft around the edges.* It was a wonderful voice, a friendly voice. Penny laughed back. Someday, maybe, she *would* ask Alice what Luella had said with her hands that day. But not tonight.

Munching her dinner, Penny watched her mother and father carefully from afar. She wondered whether they were sharing the awfulness with the people at their table—the Gulsons and Willa and a woman who must be Jenny. Then she wondered if they were sharing the wonderfulness with them too. Delia's hand seemed to be permanently fixed to her midsection, and she *did* seem to be talking to Willa a lot. Penny wanted to hear the conversation, but not enough to waste a minute of her last night with her friends.

Then Penny forgot all the serious grown-up thoughts, lost them in a gloaming game of hide-and-go-seek and too many slices of watermelon.

I will never forget this night, she thought, *not ever.* It was a deliciously fun party, and yet—as each bit of fun slipped past her, as each magic moment happened, she knew she was saying goodbye.

Watching Twent the rabbit jump around the clearing, she said, "Goodbye, Twent," softly.

Watching Duncan taste his first piece of coconut

cream pie ever, with a grin on his face and his parents looming over him, she said, "Goodbye, Duncan," into the night air.

Watching Jasper point out where an owl sat high on a branch above them, she whispered, "Goodbye, Jasper."

But Penny could not say goodbye to Luella, not even in a secret whispery way. Each time she tried, she had to close her eyes and breathe deeply. She was filled with too much—*something*. There was too much to say, so there was nothing she could say.

It was a wonderful, difficult, magical night, and it had to end. Just as everyone was sitting around the fire pit staring at the flames, listening to the music of Old Joe's fiddle and Down-Betty's guitar, Delia suddenly stood up, cleared her throat, and said, "Excuse me, everyone? Excuse me? Ahem! I have an announcement to make."

The music stopped. Penny's heart stood still. Everyone looked up at Delia standing above the fire. Everyone except Penny, who couldn't bear to watch.

"First of all," Delia said, "my family and I would like to thank you nice people for making us feel so welcome. Thrush Junction is a special place. We had no idea it would be so special, and we cannot believe our good fortune in finding it. Yet . . ."

Penny closed her eyes. She felt a flutter in her chest. She opened her eyes, looked at the fire, and tried to focus on the flames so she wouldn't cry.

Meanwhile, Delia forged ahead ruthlessly, in a strong voice that Penny could not ignore. "Yet I'm afraid I have some very sad news. When my aunt Betty left us the house, she also left us a great pile of debt, debt we cannot hope to . . ." Delia paused again and seemed to consider her words carefully.

Abbie Gulson stood up, her wild halo of curls glittering in the firelight. "Why don't you just sit down," she said in a friendly way. "There's no need! You don't have to—"

"I *do* have to," said Delia firmly, "so please, let me get this over with. You see—we're going to lose the house." She looked around at the circle of faces before her. "The bank will foreclose."

Down-Betty shouted from a lawn chair, "Delia. *Really.* This is silly. Stop fretting. You'll ruin the picnic."

"No," said Delia. "You don't understand. It isn't just *us.* I wish it were. But this affects us all. All of you. Because if we lose the house, *you'll* likely be turned out into the streets. I'm sorry. It's not what my aunt intended. But there's not much I can do."

"*We* understand perfectly," said Willa, walking over

to Delia and setting a hand gently on her arm. "It's *you* who doesn't understand. Please, *listen* to us. Here." She reached into her pocket and pulled out a little piece of paper. "Here you go!"

Penny turned away from the fire now to stare. Whatever was happening, it was nothing she'd expected.

"What?" Delia took the piece of paper and tried to read it in the uneven light. "What *is* this?"

Then the other tenants—Mr. Weatherall and Old Joe and Down-Betty and Abbie and a man who must have been Alice's father—pulled small slips of paper from *their* pockets too, and they passed them around the circle to Delia until she held a small pile of paper.

"They're checks, of course!" said Willa. "Maybe not as much as we'd *like* to give you. But a little something— to help as much as each of us can afford each month."

"But I'm not allowed to charge rent," explained Delia. "It says so in the deed."

"You're not *charging* us!" said Down-Betty.

"No, we're *giving* it," said Abbie. "Did you really think we'd all stand by and watch a neighbor be thrown out into the street? That's not how it works in Thrush Junction. Dirk can pay us back in chowchow, just like Down-Betty's been paying in cucumbers for years. And maybe *you* can teach Luella some manners!" She shot her daughter a funny, wicked look. "Lord knows I can't."

"But how did you *know?*" asked Dirk, confused.

"Penny told me," Luella called out over the fire pit. "And I told my mom, and she told the others." She turned to Penny. "Sorry for being such a snitch, but I'm not much good with keeping quiet. It's my *one* flaw."

Penny looked over at her friend, who stuck out her tongue.

Then Penny flew at Luella. Without thinking, she grabbed her and pushed her to the ground in a gigantic, crazy hug to end all hugs. It was a hug that could not be stopped.

"Thank you!" Penny whispered. "Thank you so much."

After that Delia and Dirk told everyone they were speechless about two hundred times, and everyone shook hands a lot and said, "Oh, it's nothing special," when of course it was incredibly special. Dirk decided to have "one more little drink to celebrate" and Down-Betty said she couldn't stand to watch him drink alone. Delia and Willa got lost in conversation again, both with their hands on their bellies now.

So Luella and Penny ran off to lie in the grass by themselves and stare at the stars. For a few minutes they were silent, and then Penny rolled over to look at her friend.

"Luella?" asked Penny.

"Yeah, Penny?" said Luella, rolling over too.

"I'm really, really happy we're staying. Only—"

"Only what?" asked Luella.

"Promise not to laugh?" said Penny.

Luella nodded.

"It's just—I *really* thought I was going to find the treasure."

"I know," said Luella. "At first I actually wondered if maybe you'd found a map or something and not told me about it."

Penny sighed. "No, no map. But there were—oh, I don't know—all these *signs*. Almost like foreshadowing, kind of. I guess that sounds funny, but it's how I felt. Like it was fate that we go find that treasure. Like *that* was supposed to be the end of the story. I was making these wishes that I thought might actually be coming true, and it felt—like it was my adventure, like it was my mission to fix everything."

Luella pondered this. At last she said, "But it was! You *did* fix things. You told *me*, and that was the beginning of things getting fixed, right?"

Penny shook her head. "It isn't the same. The signs all pointed to the treasure, to the cave. I could feel it."

"Well," said Luella slowly, "if we *hadn't* gone looking

for the treasure, and if you hadn't *thought* you had found the treasure, you never would have gotten disappointed and upset enough to tell us the truth, so really, the solution *was* in the cave, if you think about it the right way."

Penny tried to think about it that way. It wasn't very satisfying. "Still," she said, "it would have been nice to find the treasure. If this were a book, I would have found the treasure."

Very suddenly, Luella sat up. "Penny," she said sharply.

"Yes?" replied Penny.

"*That*," said Luella, "is the stupidest thing you have ever said."

"But—"

"Because you *don't* live in a book. Nobody does, silly. Things never happen the way they would in a book. There isn't *foreshadowing*." She shook her head.

"But I thought—" said Penny.

Luella kept on. "Problems don't always get fixed. Lots of the time things are boring and dumb for no good reason. Or even terrible. And you can't do anything about it. That's life."

Penny thought about this for a minute. Then she sighed. "I know," she said.

She thought about it some more. "Or maybe I don't," she said. "But I'm starting to, anyway, I guess."

There might have been other good things to say about that, but just then a shooting star flew through the inky darkness, causing both girls to gasp.

"Quick," said Luella, pointing at the sky. "Make a wish."

But Penny didn't.

Sprawled in the clearing beneath the big night sky, Penny looked up at the shooting star and decided *not* to wish.

Instead, she rolled over and buried her face in the grass, breathed deeply, and smelled the dirt beneath her. She reached out her arms and felt the prickling of the grass blades against her bare skin.

Lying like that, quiet and full and tired and home, Penny knew that everything was as it should be; everything was perfect.

Just like she knew that someday soon everything *wouldn't* be again.

But that was okay.

The stars weren't going anywhere.

ACKNOWLEDGMENTS

There's no way to thank everyone who helped me with *Penny Dreadful*. I have many wonderful friends. I have a supportive and loving family. I have babysitters, teachers, and colleagues who keep my world in orbit. I have the incredible people at Random House behind me. I wish I could thank all of these people by name, but I can't. It isn't possible. *That's* how lucky I am. So I'm not even going to try this time. . . .

But there are three people I *must* thank. Three people without whom this book could not have been written.

First—I need to thank my husband, Chris Poma, who makes lunch and changes diapers and rushes home from work so I can scribble madly at odd hours. I don't always appreciate him. I nag the poor guy mercilessly. But I couldn't do anything without him. He's my foundation.

Second—I need to thank my agent, Tina Wexler, who keeps me working, keeps me laughing, keeps me sane, and keeps me believing in books. She's my first reader and my best advocate, but most of all, she's my friend— an honest, kind, funny woman. I need her.

Third (and most of all)—I need to thank my editor, Mallory Loehr. A book can be a slippery thing, and this one nearly slid through my fingers, but Mallory caught it! Mallory is the kind of editor a writer dreams about, and I'm humbled by the time and energy she spent on *Penny Dreadful*. Mallory is careful but quick, supportive yet critical. She is a practical dreamer, and the clearest-eyed reader I've ever known. I owe her much.

ABOUT THE AUTHOR
AND THE ILLUSTRATOR

LAUREL SNYDER, like Penelope Grey, ran away to the mountains of East Tennessee at an impressionable age, where she (like Penelope) found a world of wonderful people, winding roads, lush foliage, and wishes come true. She now lives in Atlanta with her family, and online at www.laurelsnyder.com. Her past works include *Up and Down the Scratchy Mountains*, *Inside the Slidy Diner*, and *Any Which Wall*.

ABIGAIL HALPIN grew up drawing in a tiny town on the Maine coast. Since that time, she's lived in a faraway city and visited distant states, but never quite felt at home. With pens and pencils in tow, she moved back where she grew up: Wells, Maine. She spends her days drinking tea and illustrating; her work most recently appeared in *Maybe Yes, Maybe No, Maybe Maybe* by Susan Patron. Visit Abigail online at www.theodesign.com.